I reached the beginning of Kelly's block and looked as far up the street as I could. From what I could see he was still parked there across from her place. Watching. Waiting. I wasn't sure for what.

The man in the black XKE. Whoever he was. Whatever he wanted.

I got on his side of the street behind a tree and began to carefully make my way up the block.

The XKE was running. I was close enough to see the faint green glow of the dashboard through the rear window. I picked up a large rock that would give my punch the effect of a blackjack. For a moment I had the sense that this was all a nightmare. It had that quality. I hefted the rock again and got ready to move.

The XKE door flew open and a big bald guy wearing a fashionable leather topcoat pulled six-feet-five of himself to the pavement and put a Magnum on range with the middle of my forehead. . . .

Also by Edward Gorman
Published by Ballantine Books:

NEW, IMPROVED MURDER

ROUGH CUT

MURDER STRAIGHT UP

Edward Gorman

BALLANTINE BOOKS • NEW YORK

Library of Congress Catalog Card Number: 86-3658

ISBN 0-345-33892-8

This edition published by arrangement with St. Martin's Press, Inc.

Manufactured in the United States of America

First Ballantine Books Edition: July 1987

To my parents
for their patience,
wisdom, and love

A special acknowledgment
to Dow Mossman, who
did not know he was helping.

Mention should be made of
some very good newspeople: Dave
Shay, the Dean of Iowa newscasters;
John Campbell, Iowa's best sportswriter;
and Christine Craft, journalist.

1

THE FLASHLIGHT WENT DEAD WITH NO WARNING. No fading to dim yellow. No sputtering. Just dead.

At the moment, I was somewhere on the second floor of KRLD-TV, Channel 3, standing inside an overly starched gray uniform that bore the insignia FEDERATED SECURITY on the right bicep, and the male equivalent of "sensible" shoes, big ugly brown mothers with thick squeaky rubber soles. I'm on my feet a lot.

My first reaction to any piece of gear that won't work is to subject it to threats and ridicule. You know the routine. Shake/kick/stomp it, all the while swearing at it, until it gets so embarrassed that it starts working again. I once had a Muntz TV that this number worked very well with. Other than that, my method has been singularly lacking in success.

It was dark as hell up here, and while it wasn't horror-movie spooky by any means, it was uncomfortable even for a thirty-eight-year-old ex-cop and now security man like myself.

For one thing, the flashlight had elected to cop out in the middle of a group of cubicles that were a long way from any windows. The second floor is the executive level, which means it had closed down for the day three hours ago.

Which meant it was only slightly darker in here than in Richard Nixon's mind.

In addition to being a security man, I am also an actor. True fact. To prove it, I can show you cards from both AFTRA (American Federation of Television and Radio Artists) and SAG (Screen Actors Guild). I've been in more than two dozen commercials (three of which have been on network) an innumerable dinner-theater productions, and can be glimpsed in a Paul Newman movie playing a priest. Yes.

I mention this here because one of the dinner-theater productions I'd done was *Wait Until Dark*, the play about the blind woman stalked by killers. One thing I hadn't liked about the actress was that she overdid the blind bit—you know, banging into furniture as if she were playing bumper cars with it.

But tonight was making me change my mind. She hadn't exaggerated, at least not by much.

If you'd been an observer standing to the side and watching me try to grope my way to light, you would have heard a succession of minor crashes and a steady litany of obscenities, the American male's preferred way of dealing with virtually any crisis.

Finally, my knees sore from hitting desks, my hands twitching like the antennae on a berserk ant, I stumbled out into the hallway and over to a window that was haloed with foggy golden streetlight from below.

The fog made the light eerie enough to make me feel lost

on a different plane of existence. Real "Twilight Zone." Only the persistent squeak of my shoes kept reminding me of who and what I was.

The rest was easy. I just followed the path of windows leading to the wide staircase that swept downstairs to the lobby and the brightly lit, bustling news department of Channel 3.

Or at least that was my intention.

When I got halfway to the stairs, my eyes at last adjusting to the shadow shapes that moved in the foggy light, I heard something that froze me.

In police school you are warned over and over about dark places—about going into them unprepared. Your weapon and your flashlight, you are told, are the most important things you possess at this moment. Well, we already know about my flashlight. So, for reassurance, my hand touched the formidable handle of my Smith & Wesson. The only thing moving was the sweat draining from my forehead down my face and from my armpits down my side.

Somebody, no doubt about it, had scraped something against an uncarpeted section of flooring somewhere to my right.

My mind registered all sorts of unnecessary information: the smells of floor wax, cleaning solvent, dust; the sounds of electricity thrumming in the walls, of tires *whish*ing over rainy pavement on the street below; the play of shadows deep in the staircase.

After thumbing free the catch on my holster, I drew my weapon in a single easy gesture and turned back to the origin of the sound.

Suddenly I became aware of the desperate noise my heart was making, trapped in the cage of my chest. Goddamn, only a year off the force and I was as nervous as a rookie covering his first prowler squawk.

I was taking some deep breaths, trying to calm myself down, when the intruder made his move. He was a brief silhouette against the golden fog of window. Then he was into the shadows, running.

"Stop!" I yelled.

My command didn't have any effect. He kept running, shoes slapping the hallway, deeper and deeper into the darkness at the rear of the building.

Now my fear was gone. I was too busy to worry about being afraid.

"Stop!" I shouted again.

The *slap-slap* of his shoes. He led me down a corridor, around a corner, down another corridor, around yet another corner.

Finally I had to slump against the wall, catch my breath. For long moments I could hear only my breathing. Big wet gasps of it in my ears.

And then I heard his breathing, too.

Somewhere ahead in the gloom.

But he wasn't just panting, as I was. There were sobs intermixed.

"Goddammit," he said. "Goddammit."

It was the first time I realized I was dealing with a relatively young man. Maybe even a teenager. I pushed off the wall, following my weapon, starting for the shadows where the kid was hiding behind a door.

"I've got a weapon drawn," I said. My voice sounded huge in the darkness there. "I want you to drop any weapon you've got and step over there into the light."

A window spilled more foggy light on the floor.

The breathing again. The sobbing. The kid was crying.

"Come on now," I said.

"Fuck yourself."

I might have felt sorry for him, the tears and all, if I hadn't known from experience that he was in a very dangerous state at the moment. I'd once cornered a seventeen-year-old who'd been dealing hash. He'd slammed himself up against a wall and stood there convulsed with tears. All I could think of, being a parent myself, were the strange, sad paths taken by young people sometimes. You just hope it won't happen to your own. My pity damn near got me killed. When I got up near him, shot out a hand to put reassuringly on his shoulder, he came up with a razor blade that cost me eight stitches in my forearm.

"Come on now, into the light," I repeated to this kid on this night.

He went over into the light, but only briefly. Then he did what I was trying to prevent him from doing. Reaching the door with the electric red EXIT sign above it. The door opened onto an exterior fire escape.

He lunged for it, got it opened and dove through.

In that instant I had to make a decision: to fire or not.

"You sonofabitch," I said, not sure if I was cursing him for running or me for not firing.

I jammed my weapon back into my holster and went after him. I reached the door just as it was closing. When I slammed it open, I stepped into hell. Damp, foggy, rainy light enveloped me, thick tumbling wraiths of it. I put a hand on a wet piece of iron fire escape. Below me I heard his footsteps banging on metal rungs of ladder, down, down.

"Damn," I said.

I couldn't even see him. Just hear him.

Then I couldn't even hear him anymore.

He was gone, lost in the clouds below. I stood listening to traffic, an airplane forging ahead through the muck overhead, a distant siren. "Damn," I said again. But this time I knew exactly whose ass I was gnawing on. My own.

I was going to look like one swell security guard when I filed my report with the Federated people. Not to mention the people at Channel 3.

On the first floor, in the light, I found the muddy footprints and learned how he'd gotten inside.

A john near the newsroom had gotten clogged up and started to overflow. One of the maintenance engineers had called a plumber, who, in turn, had come over and fixed the john. The only trouble was that he had left the back door—through which he'd brought all his tools—open by laying a wrench between door and jamb. You didn't exactly need to be a brain surgeon to figure out how to sneak in.

I made all the proper reports, first to the police, second to Federated and third to a man named Sears, who was essentially my boss here at Channel 3. His official title was Building Manager. He clucked and said, "Damn, the boss ain't gonna like it. Damn." Then he hung up. The boss he referred to was a Mr. Robert Fitzgerald, station owner and local celebrity. He did his own editorials. You found him either stirring or hilarious. He could have given John Philip Sousa a few lessons in corn.

Around nine-fifty I went into the coffee room the newspeople use and had a snack from the vending machines, a purposely unhealthy one. Ho-Hos. Pepsi with real sugar. Even if it was the plumber's fault the kid had gotten in, I didn't look real good. Not with a busted flashlight and a kid who had found an easy way in and an even easier way out.

I let the news distract me.

The network show was just finishing, music up and the announcer talking about what the lucky viewer would find on the early-morning show; then suddenly there was David Curtis, Channel 3 anchorman, looking solemn as he told us what was ahead in just a few moments.

You had your basic city council scandal (the mayor was a flunky, it seemed, for every major vested interest this side of the Mississippi); you had your basic governor-at-the-ribbon-cutting-ceremony-for-a-new-factory story; you had your basic bad-news number on the Cubs (they always looked so happy; you'd think they'd have the decency to look glum at least once in awhile, the Cubbies); and you had your basic hotdog weatherman who tonight (no shit) was promising to sing "When Irish Eyes Are Smiling" in honor of his grandmother's birthday.

While the commericals were on, I looked around the coffee room. There were enough plastic chairs and tables in here to make Ronald McDonald happy for a long time. On the right was an imposing row of vending machines that sold everything from stale sandwiches to fake hot chocolate. On the left was a long bulletin board that attested to the celebrity of local newspeople. Here was Dave Curtis in his Channel 3 T-shirt making nice-nice with a heartbreakingly sad-looking little girl in leg braces; here was the singing weatherman, Bill Hanratty, leading a chorus of elderly citizens, each of whom wore a Channel 3 T-shirt; here was the ex-pro football player and now sports announcer Mike Perry in coaching togs (cap, whistle, Channel 3 T-shirt) explaining a play to a group of teenage black kids; and here was co-anchor Dev Robards, white-haired, white-bearded and Hemingwayesque, hunched over a typewriter in a pose that looked like a movie still from a 1930s tough-guy film.

There was something about the self-congratulatory air of these photographs that made me smile. From the little I'd gotten to know the Channel 3 news team (I'd been working here a week of nights), I had come to glumly to realize that that was how they perceived themselves, in some theatrical way as idealized "stars." Hey, man, Jerry Lewis helps the fuckin' crippled kids; so can we, you know?

The door opened, and in came a slender, dark-haired woman in tight designer jeans and a blue pullover sweater. With the bow in her hair she mangaed to look younger than the body pushing against the jeans suggested. Her name was Kelly Ford. She was Channel 3's news consultant.

"Hi," she said. Her voice suggested that she thought it was wonderful of herself to speak in such a nice way to the hired help. She was in her mid-forties and—despite herself and her bullshit arrogance—there was something sexy in the desperation of her dark glance and the twitchy way she pushed quarters into the Pepsi machine. You began to think the arrogance wasn't real, that it was a bluff.

"We've painted the set a new color for tonight. See what you think."

"Sure," I said.

I looked down at the empty Ho-Hos package in front of me. I noticed that she was noticing it, too. I'm afraid there is not much good you can say about a man my age who eats Ho-Hos.

"Glad to see somebody else has the same problem."

"Oh, yeah," I kind of muttered. "Junk food."

"I didn't mean to embarrass you." She stood over me, hip cocked, smiling. "But I did, didn't I?"

"Sort of, I guess. I mean personally I feel that anybody who would eat Ho-Hos is capable of doing anything."

She laughed. "Anything?"

I nodded. "Unfortunately, yes."

Then something happened to her face. The smile vanished as if she'd been kicked in the stomach. Her eyes narrowed. Her jaw locked. "Straight up," she said, glancing at the clock that read exactly ten o'clock. "The show is starting." Her transformation from chatty companion to all-business news consultant was almost terrifying in its abruptness. But then, in a real sense, this was "her" show. Or at least it was her very nice fortyish ass that was on the line.

You know how news shows open these days. All that hokey horseshit with the fast cuts and up-tempo music to show that our newspeople go out there and, by God, personally bring the news back themselves. Right.

Well, it was just after one of those standard-issue news openings when it happened. The sequence was this. First there was a shot that briefly showed the entire Channel 3 team: David Curtis and Dev Robards, co-anchors; singing Bill Hanratty, weatherman; and Mike Perry, sports. And then the director cut to the number-two camera.

That's when David Curtis, just as the camera fixed on him, got a very odd look on his otherwise handsome face and brought a hand up abruptly to his throat. A small silver circle of foam formed around his lips. His eyes bugged as he rose out of his seat. In a restaurant once I'd seen a man start to choke. Curtis looked this way now, desperate for somebody to help him.

He put the other hand to his throat—again the impression he was strangling—but before he could do anything else, he fell face first across his desk. On the screen you saw the hump of his shoulder blade and a blank Chroma wall in front of which he'd been sitting.

"Oh, my God," Kelly Ford said. "Oh, my God." The horror on her face could be likened only to films of the Robert Kennedy assassination that still haunt me. A kind of silence scream on the faces of the onlookers, the mouth pulling back, the jaw dropping down, the neck snapping . . .

"I've got to go in there," she said. "My God."

She tried to set her drink on the table, but she missed. Ice and Pepsi exploded on the floor. Not that either of us gave a damn. At the moment we had more serious things to worry about.

2 EDELMAN HAD BEEN PICKING AT SOMETHING IN HIS nose for the past twenty minutes. I was offering up a silent prayer that he would get the little bugger. I mean, here he was in charge of a very prominent homicide investigation and, in full view of many members of the press, he was walking around doing that . . . He also wore a big squeaky pair of crepe-soled shoes. Not unlike mine. Edelman is on his feet a lot, too.

An hour had passed since Kelly Ford and I had rushed from the coffee room into the news studio, where we had found three horrified members of the newsteam standing over a slumped body of David Curtis. By the time we reached him, the silver spittle that had glistened around his mouth on the screen had turned into a genuine froth. Being a former policeman and all, I probably should have been able to guess what the cause of death was, but I'd never seen anything quite like this before.

By now the studio was packed with bodies, half dangling

various forms of official identification from sport jacket pockets, the other half wiping tears from eyes or shaking heads disconsolately.

Edelman said, "I want you to tell me about the intruder again."

We were standing over by the news desk, which looked shabby compared to the image it made on camera, and Edelman was nodding to this or that piece of evidence that this or that detective had slipped into a clear plastic bag. This was how this particular conversation was going. A part of him would be nodding okay to his people, the other part would be listening to me.

So I told him about the kid. How he'd been hiding upstairs. How I'd trailed his muddy feet down to the first floor. How the muddy tracks had mysteriously stopped only a few feet from the staircase, then just as mysteriously gone back upstairs again. As if the kid had gotten scared all of a sudden and run back to the darkness and a safer hiding place. Then I told him how the kid had gotten away. It's not the kind of thing an ex-cop likes to admit.

He patted my stomach. "Acting must be treating you well." I had the beginnings of a gut. Just the beginnings.

"The wife and kids saw you in that commercial for that Guns and Ammo show. My kids said you looked just like Sylvester Stallone, except you're shorter and look like you haven't been out in the sun for a long time and look older."

I grinned. "Other than that, I'm a dead ringer for him, huh?"

"Seriously, though, it going pretty good for you?"

"Pretty good. I've got the Guns and Ammo gig starting tomorrow."

"Those assholes. I wouldn't want to get that close to 'em. Afraid what I'd do."

Maybe it's because he resembles a big sheep dog, maybe it's because he's so obviously a Good Daddy kind of guy, but whenever Edelman gets mad, people make the mistake of thinking that he's just talking, and that anybody this sweet of disposition couldn't actually hurt anybody. Right. I'd once seen Edelman break a drunk's jaw after the drunk had kneed him in the nuts with a kind of spectacular malice. Of course, typical of Edelman, he'd afterward gone to visit the guy several times in the county lockup, just to make sure he was all right.

Edelman's objection to my gig at the Guns and Ammo show was simple. Cops don't like the idea of citizens armed with grenade launchers and Uzis. You see, if the citizens go bad and need the weapons taken away, then it falls to the police officer to go do that little thing. Put police weaponry—even the stuff the SWAT guys pack—against some of the stuff people keep in their basements, and you'll soon see just what peril the police are really in these days. Gun nuts are not a cops best friend.

Edelman said, "I've never seen one before."

"What?" I'd lost track.

"Somebody killed by cyanide."

The angle of his blue gaze was tilted to where David Curtis was sprawled across the news desk. Somebody had covered him with a wrinkled plastic bag.

"You're kidding," I said.

"Huh-uh. That's what the silver stuff around his mouth was all about."

"Cyanide," I said. "That is really strange."

"Sir," a young cop said. "The medical examiner would like to speak to you a minute."

"Sure," Edelman said.

He turned away from us a moment. The young cop had

no idea what was going on, but I knew. The nose again. When he turned around, he was flicking his forefinger against his thumb and there was a certain look of satisfaction in his eyes. "Talk to you in awhile," he said to me, and strode off.

I found them in the lunchroom. Three of them and Kelly Ford, the consultant. Hanratty, the singing weatherman, had produced from somewhere a fifty of Cutty Sark, which he kept his hands on, pouring drinks with a kind of papal authority for whoever requested them.

There's an old saw about how, at a funeral, the death you're really mourning is your own. Maybe that explains the depth of our stock when someone we know goes violently. That's what I saw in their faces now—a certain unreality, as if Curtis were going to pop up at any moment and announce that it was all a gag.

I went over and got a Pepsi from the machine. By the time I turned around, I saw that Mike Perry, the ex-NFL tackle now turned sports announcer, was being restrained by Hanratty from lunging at somebody. Since Perry was glaring at me, I assumed that I was the object of his considerable wrath.

One thing movies never convey very accurately about fistfights is the drunkenness that's usually involved. Now, for instance. Ordinarily, Perry looks like one of those fading pieces of beefcake who spend a little too much time primping, the primping giving him an aura of desperation. The sunlamp tan, the enormous white teeth, the hooded black eyes, the gray-flecked curly hair—each was an element of a huge mannequin that at somewhere around forty was just beginning to show wrinkles. Football autumn was a long way behind him, but he obviously fought its loss with a kind of sad violence that he was unable to control.

Like now.

His eyes looked a little vague from booze, and his mouth was wet from spittle, and his necktie was askew. There was a jock madness loose in him, the kind that always leads star players to get booked for assault and battery during a night of drinking.

"C'mon, Mike, just sit down there," Hanratty said. Then to me, "Why don't you go somewhere, okay?"

"Yeah," Perry said. "Go somewhere before I push your fucking face in."

"Why don't you cool out, Perry? He didn't do anything."

The speaker was Dev Robards, Channel 3's co-anchor. An elegant gray-haired man who usually wore blue suits, he had been a local TV institution since I'd been in high school. He was still good, but it was obvious even to the viewers at home that he was gradually being relieved of most of his duties.

"That's the point—he didn't do anything, and that's exactly how that kid got in here and poisoned Dave," Perry snapped.

So that was it.

Whoever the kid was, he was already the number-one suspect. And it was my fault that he'd managed to get in in the first place.

Kelly Ford stood up and came over and stood next to me. "I'm sorry," she said. "They're all a little overwrought."

"Yeah."

Then Hanratty, the singing weatherman, came up. He looked like the kind of guy you used to see on Lawrence Welk singing Nelson Eddy songs updated with a vaguely disco beat. He winked at me and touched my arm. "For what it's worth"—and here he leaned in as if he were a doctor about to tell me something terrible—"we know you're in no way responsible."

"Gee, thanks."

For just a moment his head kicked back. He was obviously wondering if my gratitude might not contain just a hint of sarcasm.

"We're like a family, the whole newsteam," he said, "just like a family."

Kelly Ford stepped closer. "Thank you, Bill. Why don't I talk with him now, all right?"

She was his mother. That was the sense I'd had of her the nights I'd worked here. You remember the very pretty yet somehow remote girl in grade school, the one with neat penmanship who always got As, the one who could have been a real beauty if she hadn't been quite so square? I had the sense that this was the Kelly Ford story. This is what happened to all those girls later in life. "It's going to be all right, Bill. We're going to find out what happened and who did it, and it's going to be all right." If she hadn't talked quite so quickly, and if there hadn't been an unmistakable tremor in her voice, I might have had a bit more faith in her reassurance. She possessed one of those calming touches that seemed to have been dipped in miracle waters just recently. She used it on me now, steering me out the door before I could object.

"They're obviously very upset about this. I just didn't want you to have to suffer for it."

I looked at her and smiled.

"What's funny?"

"You. You're kind of the eternal den mother."

"I suppose it's my age coming out."

"Oh, yeah, you're a real grandmother type."

"I'm old enough to be a grandmother."

"Right."

"No, really. I am. Forty-three. There are forty-three-year-old grandmothers."

"There are also one-armed baseall players. Just not very many of them."

She smiled again. There was something about her that put me in mind of warm cotton jammies on cold winter nights.

She shook her head. "The whole week's been creepy. Ever since the break-in."

"What break-in?"

"At my office."

I was going to ask her more questions, but then I saw her head rise and a curious look come into her eyes. I wasn't sure what I was seeing—just something intense and enigmatic.

I recognized him from the tube. A short man, maybe five-six, five-seven at most, with dark curly hair worn in something resembling a crew cut. His blue blazer and open white shirt gave him the look of an executive after hours. The ferocity of his blue gaze said he was a very successful executive and did not want you to forget it. Napoleon had probably sent much the same signal. There was one thing I hadn't known about him: the catch in his right leg when he walked. He was lame.

He drew abreast of me, his upper lip curled slightly, as if my existence gave him great offense, and then he snapped his fingers and glared at Kelly and said, "My office. Right away."

When he had gone by us, she whispered, "God, this is going to be terrible."

The man we'd just seen was none other than Robert Fitzgerald himself, chief stockholder and president of Channel 3.

3

THE MEDICAL EXAMINER WAS HOLDING A PLASTIC bag up. Inside it was a white tube with the name FIBERALL across its front.

"Edelman, I'll bet you a steak dinner at Farrady's that this is how he ingested the cyanide," the M.E. said. His name was Sullivan. He was one of those doctors who didn't look like a doctor. Shabby clothes. Bald pate but dandruff anyway. Dirty nails.

"Laxative," Edelman said.

I was back in the studio. The place still resembled a telethon. The press from other channels were in now. They managed to convey the impression that this was a big deal for them. Getting to spy on the competition. The cops had only just begun. Rolls of film were being shot. Pounds of fingerprint powder were being dusted. Yards of cotton tape were being measured off. Dozens of plastic bags were being filled with items that seemed to have no bearing whatsoever on a murder investigation. But that's usually what did it for a prosecuting attorney. Some arcane little piece of physical evidence. For cops it was informers. Without informers, homicide cops would be out of business, all the clue-solving TV shows to the contrary.

"A laxative," Edelman was saying. "Christ."

"And judging from a quick look inside, I'd say that whoever did it really dropped a large amount in here, too," Sullivan said.

"Wouldn't he taste it?" Edelman asked.

"You ever use this stuff?"

Edelman shook his head.

"A dog could take a crap in it and you wouldn't notice it," Sullivan said poetically. Then he said "Hey!" abruptly to an intern doing something that was apparently not up to Sullivan's standards.

"God, I'd hate to have that guy for a boss," Edelman said when Sullivan reached the young intern and started chewing on him. Then he turned back to me. "So, you pick anything up during your week here?"

"Not really."

"Nobody who really hated this guy?"

I shrugged. "It's like any other type of show biz. They probably all hated him. He had the job they all wanted."

"Sound like nice folks."

"Probably not any worse or any better than anybody else."

He took out a pipe, put it in his mouth. It was a prop. He had given up Chesterfields ten years ago, and since then, teething-ring style, he'd adopted one of those fancy two-colored pipes. This one was red and yellow. You almost expected to see bubbles wafting up out of it. Everybody called it his "toy pipe." "I had a very pleasant conversation with Robert Fitzgerald earlier tonight."

"I just met the man."

"He seems to be of the opinion that you and the plumber, whose name is Fletcher, should be castrated and then set on fire."

I sighed. "Yeah. That's the impression I got." I shook my head. "I should have gotten him."

"Huh?"

I had muttered to myself. A sure sign of shame. I cleared my throat. "I said I should have gotten him."

"The kid?"

I nodded. "Not that I'm sure he did it."

"He'll do till somebody better comes along."

I felt singularly inept. "I just should have gotten him."

"Hell, no big deal."

"It will be to Federated Security."

"What do those guys know?" He grinned wickedly. "They're just a bunch of guys who couldn't make the cut as real cops."

"Thanks."

"Not you, Dwyer. You're a real cop."

"Gee, this is sort of like being knighted."

He put his hand on my shoulder and said, "How's that woman you were seeing?"

"Donna Harris?"

"Yeah."

"Seeing a shrink."

He looked confused.

"Her ex-husband's in the picture again. Wants her back. She can't decide what to do. So she's seeing a shrink."

"Does that mean she can't see you?"

I shrugged, trying to appear far more indifferent than I actually felt about it. That's a holdover from high school—not wanting the other guy to know how much you care about a certain girl. "It just means we're kind of not, uh, tied down to each other. You know?"

"Yeah, I know." He frowned. Tapped my stomach again. "You got a gut. Now you need a wife."

"You sure make suburbia sound nice, Martin. Sit around with the little woman and stare at your gut."

He laughed. "I worry about you, Dwyer. I really do." For all his joking, he was being serious. He did worry about me.

My shift had officially ended half an hour ago. There was no reason to stay around. By morning Robert Fitzgerald would have lodged an official complaint. By noon I would most likely be filling out job applications. Federated had an ongoing contract with Channel 3; they wouldn't jeopardize it by keeping me on payroll. They would make a very big thing to Fitzgerald about getting rid of me. I would have done exactly the same thing.

A ring of gawkers, kept at bay by police barricades, stood bathed in whirling blue and red and yellow emergency lights. There had been many more of them a while ago, but it was nearing midnight now and the wind was harsh and the novelty was wearing off. A dead local anchorman will not hold your interest nearly as long as a dead network TV star, for instance. And a dead network TV star will not hold your interest as long as a dead bona fide movie star. When you look at it in terms of a pecking order, the universe does make sense.

I recognized a couple of the patrolmen who were drinking

coffee out of thermos cups between thick gloved hands. We waved to each other, and for a moment I got sentimental as shit about being a cop. I had had some good times before an appearance in a public-service spot as a cop (what else?) got me interested in acting and led eventually to the breakup of my marriage and my leaving the force. I still couldn't say it, couldn't say, "I'm an actor," when people asked me what I did. I just said, "Security man." Sounds a lot saner.

My car was parked around the side of the building. The wind was strong enough to make me tilt into it to keep from being knocked over. I had my evening planned. Three or four beers, a sandwich made from the salami, tomatoes, mayo and dark bread in my kitchen, and then a late movie. *The Asphalt Jungle* was on KTBS. A crusher. A fucking crusher.

By the time I reached my car, a rusted symbol of the days when everybody wanted small Japanese imports, my mind was already tracking back to the murder.

I just kept remembering the froth around his mouth. His bugged-out eyes. His twisted, imploring hands. Damn it.

Channel 3 is located on the northwestern edge of the city. Encircling the new building are woods dense enough to get lost in. Just beyond the eerie touch of the mercury vapors lay trees that formed a virtual wall. And that was where I saw the flash. I was tired enough, and stressed enough from thinking about losing my job, to discount it as nothing more than a piece of stray paper tumbling in the wind.

I got inside my car, the dome light almost lurid in the night; turned on the local jazz station, which was playing one of the best collaborations ever, J.J. Johnson and André Previn playing the music of Kurt Weill; and was just backing out when I saw it again in the rearview mirror. The flash. I knew now it was not a piece of paper but rather a human being darting in and out behind the trees.

From my cop days I knew that the best thing I had going was the element of surprise.

I continued backing out, but when my car angled toward the woods to my left, I slammed open the door and pulled myself out.

Within two steps, I was running.

All of us have these hotdog fantasies. I'm no different. I'd like to rescue beautiful blondes and be amply rewarded, too. But what I was probably thinking about right now was that I was going to find some mysterious person who was lurking about in the woods and turn that person in, thereby solving the murder of David Curtis. No beautiful blondes in this case. It would just mean that I wouldn't have to find another job.

Even though I jog, running through a wintry woodscape at midnight is far tougher on the knees and hips than a track or even concrete. Especially when you've got low branches trying to dismember you every so often.

The deeper we went, the darker it got.

By now I had gotten a good enough glimpse of the person to know two things: one, it was a girl, and two, it was a blond teenager. Definitely not the kid I'd seen earlier this evening.

She flashed in and out of sight, between trees, behind tall undergrowth, tripping once, regaining her footing, tripping again, then disappearing again. This went on for ten minutes. She must have had rubber lungs.

Twice I stopped to catch my breath, to feel the sweat stand on my otherwise cold body. Then I started running again. We were headed up a steep incline, on the other side of which I could see the glow of lights from a boulevard below.

Once she turned and looked back at me, and in that moment I realized how pretty she was. Even sweat-slicked and desperate, she was fetching.

She fell again and this time let out a loud curse that was mixed with a sob. She was near the top of the hill, lost briefly behind some brambles, then scrambling on her hands and knees to the top of the rise. We were in an area where dead leaves from last fall stank sourly from dying rainwater.

Then she was gone.

It was like watching a parachutist do her stuff. One moment she's at the crest of the rise and then her hands are going up in some kind of free fall, and then she's vanished.

She would be fast footing it downhill, down to the boulevard, where a ride could be waiting or a ride could be obtained.

She wasn't going to get away from me. Not this one.

I came to the top of the rise myself and looked down onto a wide avenue where two lanes of cars moved in each direction with a kind of frustrated allegiance to the speed laws. This street was heavily patrolled. More than one teenager had lost his license on this street. I'd plied this concrete myself in a 'fifty-nine Chevy.

She was at the curb now, running alongside the oncoming traffic with her thumb out. The cars were an unending stream of glistening colors and headlights, like something glimpsed in fast-motion photography. Her blond hair flying, she looked amost posed against this backdrop, like an inexplicably erotic image on MTV.

I didn't actually see her get hit. Only heard brakes screeching on. And her scream.

By the time I looked up, scrambling down the hill, I saw her grab her leg and fall to the roadside. The way she twisted back and forth, her pain was obvious.

The car, a new Dodge convertible, had stopped, and a suburban-looking guy was running around the front of it.

"Hey!" I yelled, sensing what he was about to do.

They both looked up at me as if I'd just fired a shot. Then she screamed something at him, something lost in the roar of the traffic, something that was not too difficult for me to imagine (he's chasing me, help me, get me out of here), and then he had his arm around her waist and was helping her quickly into his car.

"No! Stop!" I yelled, running down the rest of the hill to the pavement.

But by the time I reached the concrete, the convertible was tearing away from the scene, the tires literally smoking.

What a hell of a cop I was. For the second time that night, somebody had eluded me, while a poor bastard of a newsman lay poisoned in the studios of Channel 3 and there was a dim chance that I had played at least some role in his death.

EXHAUSTION OVERWHELMED ME THE MOMENT I stepped inside my tiny efficiency apartment. When my fifteen-year-old son comes to visit me, he always takes a quick look around and says, "Hey, Dad, why don't we go to McDonald's and get something to eat, okay?" He says this without quite getting all the way inside. You don't need to, really, to get any true sense of the place. Maybe it's the urine-specimen-yellow color of the wallpaper. Maybe it's the variously ripped and rent furnishings. Or maybe it's the fact that there are no windows. A woman I used to sleep with (as opposed to be in love with or even really like all that much) once laid her head on my arm afterward, looked around and said, "I'll bet it's nicer in San Quentin than here."

Anyway, at the end of a long day during which I'd lost not one but two parts (one a voice-over for a muffler shop, the second a walk-on role in a doughnut commerical), and during which I'd ruined an otherwise good record as a security man by letting not one but two people escape my clutches, my place was not exactly the kind of haven where you went to get cheered up.

The first thing I did was check my phone service. One call. Donna Harris. "She said she'd be up watching *The Asphalt Jungle,* so call even if it's late," the woman on the service said.

"Thanks," I said.

"You sound kinda tired tonight, Dwyer."

"I am."

Then I dialed Donna.

"Boy you sound grouchy," she said.

Did I really want to relive all the bullshit by repeating it, even if she was capable of giving me world-class sympathy? I decided no.

"Been a long day," was all I said.

"Yeah, me too. The printer has decided he needs a fourteen-percent increase to keep on printing my newsletter, so I've been running all over the city trying to find somebody who'll do it for the old price."

"No luck?"

"Not yet."

"Don't worry, it's a hungry world out there. You'll find somebody."

"I sure hope so. I'm just starting to get the subscription list to really make this thing pay."

Donna writes, edits and publishes a newsletter for the advertising agencies in this state called *Ad World.* It was because of the newsletter, in fact, that we'd met several months earlier. She'd been covering a murder investigation that, together, we more or less helped bring to an end.

I'd also managed to fall in love with her, or something so

much like it that I couldn't tell the difference. There was, and remained, however, a Problem. Her ex-husband. Forget he's rich. Forget he's handsome. Forget he's manipulative. What he also is is a fucking child. He dumped her for a younger woman (Donna's in her mid-thirties), then in turn dumped the younger woman for Donna. Then he did the same thing all over again. It was a testament to his prowess that he managed to keep both these women totally locked into his games. The upshot, anyway, was that Donna was now seeing a shrink and trying to "work through her feelings," as the jargon goes.

We hadn't seen each other for two weeks because Rex, the shrink, thought she needed time to herself to see what she really felt. Meanwhile my life went on pretty much as always. By day I made the rounds at auditions, by night I worked my security-guard gig. I was nearly forty. I felt like the world's oldest teenager. This was not the kind of life the Sisters of Mercy foresaw for me.

"So how did it go with Rex this afternoon?"

"I'm beginning to wonder about him," she said. Donna was about as good at hiding her feelings as Jerry Lewis.

"What happened?"

"It's hardly worth talking about."

"You want to, though. 'Hardly' gave you away."

"What?"

"The word 'hardly.' Hardly means you want me to ask you about it. If you hadn't wanted me to ask you, you wouldn't have brought it up in the first place or you would have just said, 'It isn't worth talking about.' There wouldn't have been any 'hardly.'"

"I think he's putting the moves on me."

"Jesus."

"Really. He's started touching me a lot."

"Well, you're only paying him fifty bucks an hour."

"Funny, Dwyer. And anyway, it's fifty-five an hour."

"He raised his rates?"

"Said his bookkeeping costs went up."

"The poor dear."

"So anyway he's lost some credibility. I mean since he's gotten all touchy feely."

"I'm sorry to hear that."

"No you're not. You've always hated Rex."

"I just think he's a twink."

"I'm just sort of afraid to break the bond. I've gotten used to seeing him twice a week now."

"You'd survive."

She sighed. "I need a lot of help right now. I'm so damn indecisive."

"Gee, you could have fooled me."

"I don't know why you put up with me."

"I don't either."

"I'm serious, Dwyer."

"So am I."

She waited and then said. "You really don't know why you put up with me?"

"I was only half serious."

"Half. That still hurts my feelings."

"Okay. Make it a quarter then."

"I really miss you, Dwyer."

"I know."

"I do."

"You don't sound like you do," I said.

"God," she said.

"Are you in your bunny jammies?" I asked.

"No, when I wear them I think about you."

"There are worse people to think about."

She lauged. "Name one."

"Rex, for one."

"Okay, Rex is pretty bad to think about." I could feel her frown over the phone. "Damn, I really used to trust him."

"Actually, it's too bad."

"It is."

"Don't get so paranoid," I said. "I'm agreeing with you. Seriously. I thought you were getting somewhere with him, you know, when he explained how much Chad was acting out the role of your father, and how Chad tended to reject you in just about the same ways your father did. It all sounded very Freudian and very likely. Then Rex had to go and fuck everything up by putting the moves on you."

"It's his shoes—I should have known better."

"His shoes?"

"He wears clogs."

"Shower clogs?"

"No, you know, the wooden kind that men wear in the summer. He wears them year round."

"His name is Rex and he wears clogs. Year round. He sounds fine to me. Of course what do I know? I drink Blatz."

"You just don't like him."

"Really? What gave me away?"

I looked at the TV. *The Asphalt Jungle* was starting. I just wanted to sit down and relax and forget it all, the killing tonight and the kid on the second floor and my competence being called into question and how Donna couldn't make up her mind whether or not to finally break the ties with her husband.

"*The Asphalt Jungle* is on."

"Do you want to watch it?"

"Kind of, I guess."

"God, Rex would say you're not being demonstrative. You should just say I'd really like to watch it and then say good night and hang up."

"Fuck Rex."

"Why don't you just say you want to go?"

"Okay, I want to go."

"You don't miss me, do you, Dwyer?" She was starting to cry.

"Why don't you ditch your ex-husband and really give us a chance, Donna? I love your ass off, kiddo, I really do."

"I guess that's a decent way of putting it." Then she said, "Good night, Dwyer. I love your ass off, too."

Twenty minutes later, just when I was spreading mayo on dark bread, just when Sterling Hayden was talking about the robbery he knew he could pull off, the phone rang and a gruff male voice, Becker from Federated, said, "Seems like we'd better have a little talk tomorrow morning, Dwyer."

"Seems like," I said.

He slammed the phone down.

5 IN THE MORNING I DID MY WORKOUT WITH THE beautiful ladies on one of the cable channels (amazing how you can be punishing yourself, gasping, aching, dripping sweat, and still not lose the erotic urge you have for them), and after showering, shaving and eating my bowl of bran, I got right to work.

The teenage girl I'd chased last night now disturbed me as much as the boy who'd eluded me inside Channel 3. Why had she been hiding outside the station? Why had she run when I'd seen her?

The Yellow Pages listed eight emergency hospitals. I went through them alphabetically, asking each clipped voice if a young girl had turned herself in early this morning for an injured leg. While I did not say I was the police, I didn't exactly discourage them from thinking I was.

Call six proved lucky. A girl had shown up around one o'clock this morning, the woman said. But then she paused. She was afraid I should speak to her supervisor, which I did, much to my regret. The supervisor immediately asked my name, my relationship to the police department and the name and title of *my* immediate supervisor. I hung up.

Federated Security sits right on the edge of a ghetto. Years ago it was a house; now it resembles a kind of prison. All the windows are covered with wire mesh. The doors are slabs of metal. The cars that sit at the curb and in the driveway carry whip antennae and shotgun racks. If you look carefully, you can find smears of blood in some of the backseats.

The inside of the house looks like a graveyard for Army-surplus office furniture. Becker, who was a captain in the Marines, knows somebody in Washington and gets the stuff cheap. The lobby area always makes me smile. That's where Bobby Lee sits in her 1965 beehive hairdo, chain-smoking her Kool filters and tapping her feet to whatever country atrocity is emanating from her transistor radio. Bobby Lee was Becker's mistress and had been for at least ten years. The only person on the North American continent who did not seem to know this was Mrs. Becker, a woman I'd met only over the phone. She was pushy enough to almost make me feel sorry for Becker. Almost.

Bobby Lee obviously knew about my problem at Channel 3. She had never liked me and I had never liked her, and that accounted for her superior smile this morning.

"I hear our little lesbian got himself in some trouble last night," Bobby said.

Which should tell you all you need to know about her humor. "Lesbian" is the way she intentionally mis-prounounced "thespian." She obviously did not have a lot of faith in my acting career. She resented anybody who aspired to anything more than a blue-collar life had to offer. She blew menthol smoke my way. I've never understood people who smoke Kools. Why don't they just light up a cough drop?

Then she stood up to do some filing. She had an ass a stud horse would have been ashamed of, packed inside a ridiculously tight pair of jeans. Her T-shirt this morning read THE MERLE HAGGARD TOUR '84. The print was stretched tight over her full breasts. As she sat back down, I checked out her hair again. Somewhere in there was probably a family of birdies eating worms.

"You haven't turned your hours in yet this week, so I just went ahead and paid you. I'll put 'em on next week."

Bitch.

This was another one of our nasty little games. Or rather *her* nasty little games. She knew I was always in need of money, and so that gave her a certain petty power over me—one she rubbed my face in occasionally by doing my regular hours "early" and making sure that I didn't have time to put on my overtime hours, which usually amounted to half again as much pay. I would be strapped for awhile.

"Sorry," she said. Her smile had become a smirk.

"Yeah," I said.

Becker was waiting for me when I pushed past Bobby Lee's desk and went into his office. His place looked like a Nazi's wet dream. Becker, short, chunky, with a graying crew cut and blue contacts that made his eyes almost gaudy, was a model airplane fanatic. The Army-surplus furniture in there was covered, every frigging inch of it, with planes. The walls were covered with photographs of model planes. He even had a sport shirt made for him that was covered with planes.

He sat back and looked at me and tucked a little but obvious piece of disappointment into the corner of his mouth. That was Becker's management style. He never yelled at you. He never threatened you. He just let you know, in various ways, how much you'd let him down. Here he was suffering for your sins, and you were too stupid to realize it.

His guilt routine didn't work on me very well. Unlike the majority of people Becker employed, I have an IQ above room temperature and I don't have an erotic attachment to guns. One thing you have to realize about security people. Most of them get into the business because for some reason or other they are failed people officers, ones not bright enough or healthy enough or sane enough to wear the uniform. So they become security people for little better than minimum wage and push around citizens whenever they get the chance and are pushed around in turn by military types like Becker, who make small fortunes on them.

"Dwyer, Dwyer, Dwyer," Becker said. This was going to be a network special of disappointment.

"You talked to Fitzgerald at Channel Three yet this morning?"

"Yeah."

"And?"

"He wants me to fire you."

"Great."

"You did fuck up, you know."

"I guess I did."

"You guess?"

"Well, if I bring up the subject of the plumber who let the

kid in in the first place, then it sounds like I'm copping out."

"But the plumber isn't our problem, is he?"

Uh-oh: Here went his schoolmarm routine. "No, I guess he isn't." What could I say? I needed the job.

"You know what percentage of security jobs are lost just because of situations like this?"

"Gee, not offhand I don't."

If he picked up my sarcasm, he didn't let on.

"Forty-two per cent of security jobs are lost because of perceived incompetence. And those aren't my figures, those are figures straight from *Security Times*, our trade magazine. I've told you, Dwyer, you should read it."

Now he was shifting into his instructional phase. If you remember Bullwinkle the Moose and his Mr. Know-It-All persona, you've got this part of Becker down pat. Becker knows more about more things than anybody *I've* ever known, and that's the trouble with him—he knows the facts about everything and the truth about nothing. He's the ultimate B student.

"If you're going to fire me, let's get it over with, okay?"

He put some more disappointment on his face. "That would be the easy way out, don't you think?"

I sighed. "I don't know what you're getting at." I thought I heard Bobby Lee sneaking around behind me. She was enjoying herself. I didn't want to be her pathetic little show for the day.

"Dwyer, you're not thinking very clearly this morning."

"I guess I'm not."

"You were a detective, weren't you?"

"Yes."

"Then find out on your own who that kid was."

"So I'm not fired."

"Yes. You are."

I just stared at him.

"But if you can find out who the kid was, you get your job back."

"I need work now."

He looked at me. "Check in later. Maybe I'll change my mind." Bobby Lee was in the hallway. Eavesdropping.

"Bobby Lee, is that you?" Becker yelled.

She peeked her head in. "Yes, Earl. Why?"

He got the Look again. This time it was his own mistress who had disappointed him. "Bobby Lee, we're trying to have a private conversation here. Now I know how much you like to eavesdrop, but you know how much I don't *like* for you to eavesdrop."

She blushed. "God damn you, Earl. You have no right to talk to me in front of—*him* this way."

"It's all right, Bobby Lee, I knew you eavesdropped before he brought my attention to it."

"Why you—" she started to say.

"God damn but I wish you two got along better," Earl Becker said, sitting there amidst his toy airplanes. "You two argue like me and my goddamn wife."

The St. Francis Medical Center was one of the new buildings along the river. Spring sunlight reflected off its glass and was trapped in the green landscaping of its instant grass.

Three steps inside and I remembered why I don't like emergency rooms. An infant with scarlet cheeks and a dead gaze sat limply burning in his mother's lap; an old man holding his chest was fussed over nervously by a sorrowful frail woman, obviously his wife; an eight-year-old boy with what appeared to be a broken wrist sat in a chair while his mother did all sorts of overprotective mother things that apparently embarrassed the kid. Doctors and nurses came and went; the same soap opera played on three different TV screens.

I walked up to the crisp, pretty nurse at the registration desk and said, "My daughter left her umbrella here last night."

The nurse put down her pen and said, "Well, let me go check and see if an umbrella was left."

"Great."

While she went to look, I smiled to myself about Becker. This morning had been one of the few times I'd ever seen him happy. That was because one of his people was getting involved in actual detective work. Becker had a lot of theories about cops, mostly that they were incompetent and dishonest. I hadn't had nerve enough to give him my opinion about military men. Becker was of the opinion that I wouldn't have checked into the events at Channel 3 last night on my own. I decided not to spoil his self-image. I hadn't mentioned the girl I'd chased through the woods.

"Gosh, nobody left an umbrella here last night, I'm afraid," the nurse said when she came back.

"Darn," I said, "it's one her grandmother gave her. Sentimental attachment. You know. Especially since grandma . . ." I shrugged. My tone implied that something terrible had happened to old Grams. I left it to her imagination to decide what.

She looked down at her registration book. Something seemed to bother her. "How old is your daughter?"

I took a guess. "Sixteen." If I'd said, "Oh, sixteen,

seventeen," I probably wouldn't have sounded too convincing.

"That's funny. The only teenage girl we have listed here from last night is a Diane Beaufort. And she listed her address as Falworthy House." She offered a kind of half-frown. "Falworthy House is something between a halfway house and an orphanage."

"Boy, that is strange," I agreed. But my heart was slamming against my chest and my palms were wet. I'd gotten what I wanted, and now I needed out of here.

"Hmmm," she said, concerned-looking now. "What did you say your daughter's name was?"

I gave your a name and then I gave her good-bye. Just as I was leaving, the tiny baby with the burning cheeks erupted into a hell of pained crying.

6 FALWORTHY HOUSE HAD ONCE BEEN A THREE-STORY red-brick mansion. Now, with a cyclone fence surrounding the perimeter, it resembled one of those forbidding places in which secret government experiments are conducted. Not even apple blossoms and a sweet gentle breeze helped.

The front gate had to be buzzed open and to get inside you had to identify yourself, which I did. Then I added, "I'm here to talk about one of your people who may be in some trouble."

I was buzzed inside.

On the broad two-stepped concrete porch sat several teenagers eyeing me with a mixture of contempt and irony. You remember what it's like being a teenager—nobody knows shit but you. Like that.

When I reached them, I nodded to a boy wearing a long earring and green-tinted hair. He glared back at me.

Inside was a vestibule big enough to house a hockey

game. The decor was vintage seventies. Lots of ferns and posters with various Love messages. From a room upstairs came the sounds of a Donna Summer disco record. The place was stuck in a time warp.

The small nervous man who seemed to jump out of one of the nearby doors came right up to me and said, "You're here about the student in trouble?" He was obviously unhappy, maybe even a bit frightened.

"Yes."

"Won't you come in my office?"

He was balding and he wore rimless glasses and he moved as if he had an arthritic ache in his joints. The weird thing was I'd bet he wasn't more than forty. And to complement the seventies motif, he wore a pair of genuine bell bottoms along with one of those wide belts that had once belonged to the counterculture but were now affected by the likes of Wayne Newton.

His office was a monk's cell. Paperbacks of all kinds were jammed into bare pine bookcases. A poster of Thomas Merton stared myopically down on us. Dirty sunlight fell through a dirty window onto his desk, in back of which, along a windowsill, were arranged half a dozen Diet Pepsi cans filthy with cigarette butts and ashes.

"Who is it?" he asked, pushing his glasses up his tiny nose.

"Who?"

"The student. You said you were here about a student."

"Well," I said, "I'm actually not sure about the name. And it isn't one student, it's two."

"Two?"

"Yes. A boy and a girl."

He glanced up at the Thomas Merton poster as if for

guidance. "I see." He said this as if I'd just hit him as hard as I could in the stomach. He sank into a chair and stared out the dirty window. "We won't be open in another six months."

"Beg pardon?"

"Another six months, I said," he replied, still staring out the window. "Right now in the city council there's this big battle going on about Falworthy, about rezoning so we can't operate here. And it's exactly this kind of thing that's going to get us run out." He shook his head miserably. He had very fine, almost babyish hair and a somewhat petulant upper lip that was trying very hard to grow a mustache. Very hard. "If they only understood that I'm doing this for them," he said. He shook his head some more, and I had the uncomfortable impression for a moment that he was going to cry. Then I really wouldn't know what the fuck to do. He turned back to me. "You'll have to excuse me. I've had a hard week, I'm afraid." He put out his hand. "Karl Eler. With a *K*."

We shook.

"Would you like a Diet Pepsi or coffee or something?"

"No thanks."

He looked at me with ice-blue eyes. "Then I guess we might as well get it over with."

The quavering lip and the desperate gaze were making me wish I hadn't come.

"First of all, let's discuss what they did. That way maybe I can help you find who they are."

"Actually, I'm not sure they did anything."

For a moment, just a moment, a smile seemed to play at the edges of his prissy little mouth. Then he tensed up.

"Maybe we'd better talk about you before we talk about them."

"Me?"

"Yes, I'd like to see some ID if you don't mind."

"Sure."

I got out my wallet and handed it to him. He looked at my Federated Security card for a long time.

"So just what does this entitle you to?" he asked.

"Exactly nothing. I mean, you could throw me out. The only thing is, if you do I'll go straight to the police and tell them what I know."

"Know about what?"

"About two Falworthy students being at Channel Three last night when David Curtis was being murdered."

"Oh, my God," he said. "Oh, my God."

During the next ten minutes I told him everything I knew. I described the boy as best I could, though I hadn't really gotten much of a good glance at him, and then I described the fetching blond girl and how she'd been injured and how she'd turned herself in to the emergency ward early this morning.

"The name I got on her from the hospital was Diane Beaufort," I said. "It could be a phony."

"No. It's her real name."

"Care to tell me about her?"

He shrugged. "I suppose this is a terrible thing to say, but they're all kind of interchangeable here, really. I mean, she's from a broken home, her mother an alcoholic, her father doing time. That describes at least half of the kids here. She's had various emotional problems in the two years she's been here, the most serious of which, as far as the law is concerned, being some shoplifting trouble she got into. Kids do that. Steal as a way of punishing themselves, hoping to get caught. Anyway, Diane isn't any more or less crazy than anybody else in this place"—he smiled with a certain bitterness—"including me. My wife left me a year ago, and I guess I still consider myself one of the walking wounded. She lived here with me—we had kind of an apartment upstairs—but finally she couldn't take it anymore. The kids. Always getting in trouble, I mean. She met this professor of sociology." He twisted his lips bitterly. "I've personally always thought sociology was nothing more than quackery."

He was into himself now, which was probably good for him, but I was in a hurry. "What would she be doing at Channel Three?"

"Throwing rocks at the windows, maybe. Or writing something ugly on one of the executives' cars. She blames them, of course."

"Blames Channel Three?"

"Umm-hmm."

"For what?"

He looked at me as if I were the worst kind of bumpkin. "For playing a role in Stephen's death."

Maybe I was a bumpkin. I had no idea what he was talking about. "Who's Stephen and how did he die?"

"Stephen Chandler. He was a student here. He was one of the subjects for Channel Three's report on teenage suicide, and he killed himself. Many of the kids here blame Channel Three."

So it made sense, after all.

I was sitting in this grubby little room, listening to this sad little guy, wondering what the hell last night had to do with a halfway house for teenagers, when he just handed me the whole thing.

I knew the answer to the next question before I asked it, but I wanted to hear him say it. "Who was the reporter who handled the suicide story?"

"Oh, it was a very big story. Ran five nights. David Curtis was the reporter. You didn't see it?"

"No. I usually work nights."

"Ran about two months ago. Very popular. There were editorials in the paper, even, praising the show, pointing out how Stephen's suicide, coming as it did in the middle of the series, proved how serious the subject really was."

"Poor bastard," I said.

"Yes, yes, he was," Eler said. "Though I guess I wouldn't express it quite that way."

Which was when I pegged him for what he was—a kind of perennial grad student and perennial seminarian rolled into one. His wife's exit was making more and more sense.

"You know, back in the sixties," he said, "we really were trying to change things, make it better for the next generation. I'd say it's worse, what with all the drugs and all the sexual diseases. AIDS is crossing over to us straights now. And it may be only the first of several diseases like that."

Now I knew where I'd go anytime I needed to get cheered up. I'd just pop in on old Karl Eler (Karl with a *K* to his friends) and have him lay some good vibes on me.

"Is Diane here?" I asked.

"No. She's out."

"When will she be back?"

"Diane?"

"Yes," I said.

"Sometime this evening. She has a job after school."

"I'll be here." I paused. Watched his eyes. "You figured out who the boy might have been?"

"Mitch."

His candor surprised me.

"Mitch?"

"Mitch Tomlin. He was Stephen's best friend."

"I see."

"Took it very hard. Lots of bitterness."

I nodded. "Will he be here tonight?"

"Should be."

I stood up. Put out my hand. "Thanks for your help."

"There's just one thing."

"What's that?"

"I guess I don't understand your part in all this."

I smiled. "Neither do I. Not exactly, anyway. It's probably as simple as me trying to save my job."

He glanced around. "Believe me, I've had days when I'd just as soon lose mine." The prissy lips again. "If I had, my wife would be with me today."

He walked me out to the front porch. The same kids sat there, waiting to glare at me as I went down the steps. I felt sorry for them—they had been shit on probably since birth—and then foolish for being so sentimental. Or was I being foolish?

In a phone booth two blocks and ten minutes away, I said hello to Kelly Ford, and then, "I've made a connection between the kid in Channel Three last night and Curtis's murder."

"You have?"

"Yes. A show the station did on suicide."

"My God, that's right," she said. "The police asked us so many questions last night, and that subject didn't come up even once. At least I didn't mention it."

"Well, it sure sounds worth pursuing."

"Yes, it does. Are you going to call your friend Detective Edelman?"

"Later on. I thought we might have lunch first."

"You and me?"

"You and me."

"That's sounds very nice."

"Good. How about The Pirate's Perch in an hour?"

"Fine."

The Perch was one of the places where all the media folks lunched.

"See you then."

"Yes," she said in her nice suburban way. "And aren't you the lucky one, too?"

My weakness. Wise-ass women.

Three blocks later I swung my car over to another drive-up phone. I turned down the Neil Young song ("Old Man," one of his best), picked up the phone and dialed the number of Edelman's precinct. The guy had a right to know what I knew. Didn't he?

I kept asking myself this question while the desk sergeant put me on hold and then put me through to Edelman's office, where his secretary put me on hold. Which was when I hung up. Apparently I didn't think he *did* have a right to know. At least not yet.

7 "YES?"

The landlady looked very tired, and I suspected I knew why. Tenants of hers would seldom get themselves killed, especially prominent ones. I showed her my Federated ID. "I'd just like to talk to you a little bit."

"About David Curtis?"

"Yes."

She sighed. She was very good at it, managing to convey the impression that she was being put upon and was used to being put upon. It nicely put me on the defensive, as if my dime-store cop ID hadn't done that already.

She was maybe in her early fifties, wearing a tan pants outfit with a frilly white blouse. Her hair, makeup and nails had been done with reverence. She had undoubtedly been a beauty once, but those days were almost gone. She preserved what was left with expensive clothes and an angry dignity.

She pointed me to a chair, then handed me a discreet

white business card with her name, Bernice Weldon, printed discreetly in black. She was a protector, Bernice was, of her tenants and of an era as dead as a ballroom where Tommy Dorsey once played. I liked her without quite admiring her.

We sat in a sun-bright room filled with tasteful but bland contiental furniture. On the other side of a large window I could see dozens of cars, the least expensive being a new red BMW. David Curtis had not exactly suffered for his art.

"May I ask," she said, "why you're interested in his death?"

I was better at lying then I liked to think I was. I said, "One of his relatives contacted me."

"His parents?"

Now it was my turn to sigh. "I'm sure you're trustworthy, Mrs. Weldon, but we have to keep these things confidential."

"Yes, I suppose you do."

"All I'd like to know, really, is if anything strange or out of the ordinary happened in the last few weeks or so. To David Curtis, I mean."

"Two things, really." I got my reporter's pad out and poised my pencil. "And last night, after I saw what happened on the news, I started thinking about them."

I nodded. She was going to give me a prelude before she gave me the facts. A hearty man in a suede sport coat walked past the big window and waved inside. Bernice Weldon waved back. "We have some very nice tenants here."

"Yes," I said, hoping I didn't sound too impatient. "You were saying, about two things?"

She sighed. "The car thing, I suppose, was the most disturbing."

49

"Car thing?"

"A man in a black car was waiting for David one night. I happened to be carrying some trash out to the dumpster in back. And I saw it. The man got out of his car and then went over to David, and they talked briefly and then David tried to hit him. A punch, I mean."

"Had you ever seen this man before?"

"No."

"Could you describe the car?"

"Black."

"I know. But I mean—"

"You mean the make?"

"Yes."

"Foreign. Expensive. One of our tenants had one once. An XKE I think."

"A black XKE."

"Yes."

"How about the man? Did you get any kind of look at him?"

"Very big, bald." She thought a moment. "Sinister would be a good word."

"Could you approximate his age?"

"Perhaps forty?" She made it a question.

Another tenant walked by the window and there was another exchange of waves.

"How did their confrontation end, Mrs. Weldon?"

"They were swearing at each other—I'm glad none of the other tenants were outside to hear—and then the bald man got in his car and drove off."

"And David Curtis?"

"Well, he just stood there as if he were stunned. For a long time. Then he drove off, too."

50

I went to another page in my notebook. I wanted to signal Mrs. Weldon that things had to move along quickly. I'd driven over here more or less impulsively, thinking I had time to work in this appointment before I was to meet Kelly Ford at The Pirate's Perch.

"How about the second incident?"

"Oh, yes, right."

I poised my pencil again. I was getting good at this stuff.

"That involved Perry, Mike Perry."

"The sports announcer?"

"Yes."

I wrote his name down.

"In the lobby three nights ago they got into a terrible shouting match."

"Curtis and Perry?"

She nodded.

"You wouldn't happen to know why, would you?"

"A woman. Perry's woman. Marcie Grant. A real beauty. Anyway, it was about her."

"She had been seeing Curtis, I take it?"

She flushed, laughed. "Eventually, they *all* saw Curtis. He was quite the ladies' man." Her laughter told me that she was fascinated and repelled by the man at the same time.

"I see. How did that end?"

"With Perry stalking off. Very angrily. A few minutes later I heard a crash. Perry had put something through David's windshield."

I dutifully wrote that down.

"I warned David about these incidents, of course. We have a very pleasant type of people here. They're not used to violence of any kind."

I nodded. "Can you think of anything else, Mrs. Weldon? I mean, you've been very helpful and I hate to push you, but—"

"Not really. Except she came up the other night, late, and there was a little bit of a scene."

"Who?"

"Marcie Grant."

"What kind of scene?"

"Spurned-lover things. You know. She slammed his door and he ran after her down the hall and then he finally just let her walk out."

"Nothing else?"

"No. I'm sorry he's dead—he was a decent young man over all—but I was afraid I was going to have to evict him anyway."

"All the trouble lately?"

"Yes."

I stood up, we shook hands and before I got to the door, she was back to waving at elderly people on their way to the snug confines of Cadillacs and Continentals and Mercedes-Benzes.

When I opened the door, she said, "There was one thing about him living here, though."

"What's that?"

"He was a celebrity, and whenever I told prospective tenants about him, they seemed inpressed."

That didn't seem to say a whole hell of a lot for her prospective tenants.

8 WHEN YOU TALK TO VERY OLD THEATER PEOPLE WHO grew up around here, they tell you about an opera house built in the 1880s and torn down just after WWII to make way for a boom in downtown building. The opera house was located on the east shore of the river that divides the city. When you look at the street now it is difficult to imagine the livery stables and the trolley car system and the mercantile agency you always see in pen-and-ink drawings of the early city. There remains one relic of the era, a two-story brick building that has seen any number of hopeful restauranteurs try but fail to make a living here. Its present owners call it The Pirate's Perch. On the second floor you can look out stained-glass windows, and at dusk sometimes it is not difficult to imagine people stepping smartly from coaches in front of the opera house. But now the population is nearly a quarter-million and the industry runs to high-tech and there is not a lot of use for coaches or opera houses.

Now, at noon, the place was crowded with people too busy with gossip to notice the river that occasionally splashed the big windows at the rear of the place.

"Mind if I join you?"

I turned to see Dev Robards, looking today like a lord of the manor strolling his grounds outside Dublin. With his white hair tucked beneath a wool golfing cap, his broad shoulders pushed inside a Harris Tweed sport coat and his beard giving him a professional air, he gave the impression of a wry superiority.

He came up to the bar, and when the man behind the counter saw him they exchanged a most curious glance, communicating something far too complicated for me to understand.

"What'll it be today, Mr. Robards?"

"Oh, I think I'll coast a little. Why don't I have a ginger ale for starters."

"Sounds like a very good idea, Mr. Robards."

Robards smiled at the man, then turned back to me. Between the little exchange of dialogue and a good hard look at him in daylight, I saw his problem. He was sweating a lot, but it was more than heavy tweeds on a spring day; his fingers twitched, but it was more than nervous habit. All I had to see was how he gripped the glass of ginger ale the bartender set down to know that my suspicions were correct.

He sipped the stuff as if he knew it was going to taste very bad indeed, and then he said, "Good stuff, ginger ale."

Christ on the cross couldn't have looked much sadder.

I used to visit a buddy on a detox ward, and that's how I knew the look in the eyes. It's hope and horror at the same time—hope you can hold out against the hootch, horror that you're not strong enough.

He put a smile on his face, but his eyes still had the haunted look. "I suppose I'm number one."

"Number one?"

"Number-one suspect, of course. I had the most to gain from Curtis's death."

"Oh, I see."

"You mean you hadn't actually thought about me that way."

"I supposed I had."

He looked like hell, and I wanted to be away from him. I'd had an uncle like him, a Schlitz man who bumper-pooled and juke-boxed his life away in union bars until the Camels took his lungs and he held my hand there in the hospital, his woman long gone, and said, "I'm so fuckin' scared, Jack. I'm so fuckin' scared." And I was scared watching him, just as I was scared now in the forlorn presence of Dev Robards. You don't like people who remind you of how little you can do for anybody else.

I had to say something. I said, "So you were with Cronkite?"

He smiled sadly. "Oh, well, the station makes more of that than there really was to it. In 1952 I left Korea and got a job with CBS in New York, and one of my duties was to help Cronkite get ready for the forthcoming political conventions."

He was right about the way the station played it. According to their commercials, Walter practically owed his career to Dev Robards.

"Of course," he said, "that's how news consultants have changed our lives."

I was curious. "You don't like Kelly Ford?"

He shrugged. "Oh, personally, I like Kelly a great deal.

It's just her job, how her employers make her treat news like show business. She works for Linda Swanson, you know."

From what I knew of news consultants, he was right. They generally have two offices, one at their real place of employment, and an informal one at the TV station they're assigned to, all so that they can know the daily problems better and offer more educated answers. That's the theory, anyway.

As for Linda Swanson, she was legendary or notorious. You had your choice. She had turned happy news into an even more frenzied affair than it had been originally— goony byplay among the newsteam, stories that did not exceed one minute in length, and the depiction of a world that would have been too sweet even for Bambi. There was poverty and corruption and despair in this town, but not according to most reports on Channel 3. Instead of the homeless you saw roaming the streets, you got a guy in his suburban basement who had a big model-train layout. Instead of the chicken-shit goings-on in city politics, you got cheerleading tryouts at a local high school. Except during ratings periods, of course. That was when the mayor was questioned for his various insufficiencies, and that's when stories such as the teenage suicide one came into being. Real news was good only when it got you ratings.

"I'm sure that's why Cronkite got out when he did," Robards said. "Those dandies in the news consultancy business have even turned the networks into happy news. Look at Rather. The way they've got him sitting up so straight and all those eye smiles into the camera. It's ludicrous."

I smiled. I liked the bastard. "You don't sound like the number-one suspect to me."

"Why's that?"

"You don't sound like you want to stay in this business much longer."

He sipped some more ginger ale. "Ah, but you can't discount ego." He looked out the wide window at the sun-tipped water. "My wife died ten years ago. It was one of those stupid, impossible things. She went to the grocery store and was broadsided in an intersection. Since then I've gotten very old." He put his weary blue gaze on me. His cheeks were still sweaty. The fingers on his right hand still twitched. "Now all I have left is my ego. And I have to admit, as I'm sure others will tell you, that it hasn't been easy for me, watching Curtis take over my previous position. I used to be number one in this town. I suppose it would have been easier to accept if I'd had any kind of personal life, but—Well, anyway, Curtis was just the kind of pretty boy Linda Swanson wanted." I didn't doubt the bitterness in his voice. "At least, that's what she said her research proved."

"You doubt her research?"

"Over the years, I've become friends with several consultants. Once in a while they've told me horror stories about their field—how research gets doctored to prove a certain point; how people in the field are too lazy to get the forms filled out properly so they just fill them out themselves; the way they always blame the stations for their own failures. The consultancy business is a real racket—very low overhead, extremely high profits and practicaly no accountability, not when you can keep fixing the blame on the very people who hired you."

"The research is really altered?"

"Oh, not necessarily in the way you might think, but

subtly. Consultants tend to know the answers they want in advance, so they do everything they can to subtly influence the outcome. It's like the news itself—it's as if Spiro Agnew came back from his grave and became the news czar. Remember how he used to bitch about there not being enough 'good news' on the air? Well, the consultants saw a way of getting themselves hired if they followed that formula, and that's what they did. They convinced station owners that newspeople weren't the best judges of news stories—hell, what did journalists know, all they were interested in was the facts—while these people with their so-called research knew how to give the public what it *really* wanted . . . happy news. The news consultants invented a job for themselves and took it."

"Free enterprise."

"Bullshit is more like it."

A woman's voice. "God, why do I feel I'm taking my life in my hands by stepping up here?"

I recognized her voice instantly, and even before I turned around, I felt an unmistakable little thrill.

"Hello," she said.

Kelly Ford was dressed in a blue jersey jumper that gave her middle-aged body the look of a much younger woman. Dev Robards grinned. "I was just boring him to death with my stories of what shits news consultants are."

"With the exception of me," she said brightly.

"With the exception of you, of course."

She leaned in and kissed him on the cheek, and it was plain that there was an easy affection between the two. Only for a moment did something serious pass across her dark eyes. She looked carefully at the glass he held in his hand.

"It's ginger ale, don't worry." He smiled.

"You're doing very well, Dev. You should be proud."

"You know, I damn well am proud," he said, "now that you mention it."

"Why don't you join us for lunch?" Kelly asked, and for a terrible moment I thought he was going to say yes, he would join us.

He looked at his ginger ale, killed it and said, "Actually, I have to go out to a grade school this afternoon and talk about news."

"Nobody knows more on the subject than you," Kelly said.

He grinned devilishly. There was something boyish about it. "I have research that proves otherwise."

"He's incorrigible." She laughed.

He put down his glass, straightened his golf cap, kissed Kelly on the cheek and then walked away, looking even more now like the lord of a manor outside Dublin.

"The public doesn't want hard news," Kelly Ford told me fifteen minutes later, after Robards had left, after a college boy dressed up like Captain Kidd served us our lunch, after what seemed like half the men in the place waved over to Kelly with apreciative, horny smiles. I had asked her about Dev Robards's accusations. "Dev is a wonderful newsman," she said. "But times have changed. People don't have the appetite for hard news they once had. They seem to demand controversy instead of a simple presentation of the facts. It's a different era from the one Dev grew up in. Today viewers like to be amused and titillated."

"I suppose. But that doesn't mean that I want to spend my time looking at stories about model-train collections and barbershop quartets, either."

"Teenage prostitution," she said.

"What?"

"Teenage prostitution."

"What does that mean?"

"If I'd been videotaping your face, I could show you how interested you suddenly got in our conversation. And that's how viewers respond. Very interested."

"So that's how the teenage suicide story came about?"

"Exactly."

By now, of course, I'd figured out who she was. This morning while I'd been doing my pushups, I'd been watching a rerun of "The Mary Tyler Moore Show," and there she was, Kelly Ford. I'd been wondering what had happened to Mary now that she was in her forties. She'd said piss off to Lou and gone into the news consulting business, great looks and all.

"Well, some of the kids at Falworthy House think that David Curtis went too far." I'd already told her about my visit with Karl Eler. About seeing Diane Beaufort and Mitch Tomlin at Channel 3 last night. Maybe Curtis's death had been the result of Stephen Chandler's suicide. "They seem to think that you people would do anything to make a story sensational."

She touched a perfect finger to her perfect temple and in so doing made me realize that I was in bad need of being with a woman. Donna Harris and I had not exactly had a wonderful sex life since she'd been debating what to do about her ex-husband. I needed more than sex, of course, I always do, and in the dark shining gaze of Kelly Ford I suspected I'd find it. But there was the business at hand and I had to keep pushing.

"So you think that this Tomlin boy may have killed

David?" she said. Whenever she mentioned the death, her eyes pinched just a bit.

"Maybe. But only one thing bothers me about that."

"What?"

"The muddy tracks the kid made inside Channel Three last night."

"I don't understand."

I signaled for another round.

"You were saying," she said.

"The door the plumber left open, the door Mitch Tomlin snuck in, was a rear entrance with a flight of stairs to the second floor. The kid must have heard somebody coming as soon as he got inside and got up the steps. After Curtis died, I went back and checked out his tracks. He hid on the second floor, then started downstairs at some point. But that must have been when I went upstairs. So he had to run back up to the second floor and hide. His tracks on the first floor went only as far as the lobby. He didn't get near Curtis's dressing room. Not even close to it. It's hardly conclusive proof, but it makes me wonder."

"Have you told this to the police?"

"Not yet. My friend Edelman hasn't charged anybody, and I really don't have anything to tell him so far."

"But you sound like you don't think it was the Tomlin boy."

"I don't know. That's why I asked you to lunch. I wanted to ask you a few more questions."

She laughed with great girly poise. "Gee, so much for romance."

We let our eyes touch, and there amidst the clang and clatter of a noontime lunch, I prayed a lustful prayer that she felt at least a twinge of what I was feeling.

"What about the suicide? Do you think Curtis pushed things too far?"

She sighed. "I'm not sure what you mean by 'too far.' I really wasn't involved in the story that closely. I originated the idea with the news staff—one thing consultants try to do is feed clients ideas—but a young woman named Marcie Grant was the actual producer." She sighed again. "I do know that of the five teenagers who were interviewed, Stephen Chandler was the most volatile. David interviewed him three times, and two of those times Chandler tried to hit him. The other time Chandler broke down sobbing, saying that he didn't want to live."

I'd heard my own teenage son sob a few times. You never forget the sound.

"There's a scientific theory that states that sometimes, when you observe certain things, you alter them—just by looking at them. Maybe that's what we're talking about here," she said.

"You mean just by focusing on Chandler's past suicide attempts, Curtis brought it on?"

She nodded. "Yes. Nothing evil on his part. He just asked questions that made the boy relive certain things in his life. And the memories were so bad, the boy killed himself."

Of course, there would never be a definitive answer about that. Lots of sad kids killed themselves in this country. It was becoming a chronic problem. The kid next door with the freckles and the nice suburban parents and the secret terrors. One day he's mowing the lawn, next day his inscrutable altar-boy face is peering out of a casket. The only difference in the Chandler boy's case was that he didn't have parents. The only people who mourned him were the scruffy kids of Falworthy House, strong suicide candidates themselves, particularly with a fading, bitter flower child like Karl-with-a-*K* Eler as their leader.

"You think I could talk to Marcie Grant?"

"I'm sure you could," she said. She lifted her beautiful chin to the bar. "She's sitting over there."

Marcie Grant was in her late twenties, blond in an almost intimidating way and surrounded by enough men to look like the star of a hair-spray commercial.

"It's all right if you say wow or something," she said.

"Not my type, actually."

"Really?"

"Yeah."

"I thought that Marcie was every man's type. She's really beautiful."

"I like women with a little more dignity."

She laughed. "Boy, that's a new one. Dignity."

"Really. Women who carry themselves with a certain grace."

"Ingrid Bergman."

"You're really shrewd. Ingrid Bergman exactly."

"Well, I suppose Marcie doesn't have that." Then she smiled again. "But that's all she doesn't have."

"You know anybody who drives a black XKE?"

"Are we back to questions about the murder?"

I nodded.

"No, I don't," she said.

I decided to ask her about Curtis's landlady's story of Curtis and sports announcer Mike Perry arguing. "Aren't Marcie Grant and Mike Perry involved?"

"Does this have anything to do with a black XKE?"

"Maybe."

"You really jump around when you question people. These aren't trick questions or anything, are they?"

I smiled. "Not that I know of."

"Good. Because I've never been good at trick questions. I could never even figure out riddles."

"I just want to know about Marcie Grant and Mike Perry."

"It's difficult to keep track. They have a very mercurial relationship. Off and on all the time. But right now, no."

"Not that I know of."

"Were you aware that she was seeing David Curtis?"

"There's no way to say this without seeming catty, but Marcie has a genuine appetite for sex and men, men of all types. So, to answer your question, no I wasn't aware that she was seeing David, but it doesn't surprise me."

"How about Curtis himself?"

For some reason her cheeks flushed slightly. "What about him?"

"What was he like?" The blood remained, tiny roses on her cheeks. I said, "You're blushing."

"You could be a gentleman and not point that out."

Her putdown was worse than a slap and well deserved.

"Now you're blushing," she said.

"You had an affair with him?"

"Oh, I wouldn't call it an affair. We never went to bed or anything. It was more like a high school flirtation. We even left notes for each other. He was intriguing, I'll say that for him. I was hoping he'd get my mind off somebody else I'd been seeing for a long time but, unfortunately, he didn't. He got bored when he realized that I wasn't going to sleep with him. I'm afraid I'm really a very foolish woman. Fortunately for me, I was already brokenhearted when I began seeing him, so he couldn't really get to me."

I reached over and touched her hand, and then she smiled with the brilliance of at least a minor sun.

"Thanks," she said. "That was exactly the right thing to do."

"So he wasn't exactly a wonderful guy, huh?"

"No. He was ambitious, successful, polished, but he wasn't wonderful." She laughed. "Definitely not wonderful."

The pirate captain came back then and told us all about dessert, which we both declined.

She put her head on her palm and looked toward the sky showing in the long rear window. "It's such a perfect day. I wish I didn't have to go back to the office."

"I know what you mean."

"I didn't sleep well last night."

I yawned, as if in sympathy. "Murder has that effect on people."

"It wasn't just the murder. I'm also concerned about files being taken from my office last week."

"Right. You were going to tell me about that."

"Nothing much to say, really. I came to work one morning and several key research files were gone."

"Who would have an interest in taking them?"

"Newspeople who were concerned about their jobs, wanting to see how well they tested during phone interviews with viewers."

That interested me. "Were there any big losers?"

She frowned. "That's why we're all nervous around my office. The whole team except for David looks pretty bad. Especially Dev Robards. Then there was one other file, the one that outlined all the changes we'd be making in the next six months. Our competition would love to get their hands on it."

"You think they'd go that far?"

She put out a slender wrist and slender hand and picked up a water glass. "Sure they would. It would be valuable information. You now how competitive news operations are. If they got ahold of such a file, they'd know how to play against us perfectly."

"No ideas about who took it?"

She shook her head.

"No idea."

Suddenly there was the same half-shocked look I'd seen on her face when Robert Fitzgerald appeared last night. Now the expression was back and so was Fitzgerald. I had the sense that I didn't need to ask whom she'd been heartbroken over before David Curtis had come into her life. The only people who can inspire the expression Fitzgerald did in her are people who've had at your heart with a can opener.

Today he wore a blue pin-striped three-piece suit. With his curly black hair and mesmeric blue eyes, he might have been a B-movie version of the young Tony Curtis. Except for two things: the right leg he dragged around like something dead, and the bitterness of his gaze.

He stood two feet from our table and without even glancing at me said to her, "You pick some damn strange lunch companions, Kelly."

The blush was back on her cheeks. Worse, there was a real sense of a trapped animal in the way her hands fluttered and her shoulders sagged. I wanted to hold her, help her somehow.

She said nothing. Just put her face down. Said absolutely nothing. I couldn't believe it.

"Damn strange," he said, and limped away.

She waited a full minute and then she was up, knocking against the table, her eyes glistening with tears. "I'm sorry," she said. "I'm going back to the office."

Then she was gone, leaving me with the extraordinary echoes of her relationship with Robert Fitzgerald. I felt ashamed for her and enraged for her and utterly helpless.

He came back and grabbed me by the arm. He had a grip that could make you weep. "You stay out of my business and her business and the station's business," he said.

"Something's going on," I said, "and I'm going to find out what no matter what you say."

"You don't know who you're fucking with, bud," he said, and left again.

9

IN THE SUNLIGHT SHE LOOKED EVEN MORE BEAUTI-
ful, even more overripe and spoiled. I'd followed
her out of The Pirate's Perch and into the parking
lot and right up to her brand-new red Firebird.

At first she didn't seem to recognize me, but then as she
realized who I was, she looked as though I'd just handed her
a paper bag containing doggie-doo.

"Jesus," she said, "you followed me out here to put the
shot on me?" She threw back her blond hair with a model's
melodramatic air. Her question, an epic of immodesty,
made me smile. For a moment Marcie Grant couldn't
imagine, just couldn't imagine, that anybody of the male
sex would want something other than to hump her.

"I wanted to ask you about Mike Perry."

"Why?"

"Why what?"

"Why do you want to ask me about Mike Perry?"

"Because there are some things I need to know."

"You're that security guard aren't you?" She managed to make it sound like, You're the guy who burns down orphanages aren't you? It was then—I'm a slow learner—that I realized why Marcie Grant had the most violet eyes, almost glowing eyes, of any I'd ever seen before. She wore violet contact lenses.

"Yeah," I said.

She opened her car door.

With speedboats on the river, warm and rich sunlight bathing nearby apple blossom trees and newborn grass blinding you with its green everywhere, this should have been a very nice moment.

Her sneer made it otherwise.

She got into the car, slammed the door shut and started the considerable engine. As she slipped it into gear I knocked on the window. I'd been in a similar situation years ago with my wife during an especially bad argument. She'd backed over my foot and roared away. Now I kept my foot out of Marcie Grant's way.

She surprised me by rolling down the window. "Did I ever tell you about the story I produced on security people?"

"I guess not."

"You people are cretins. Cretins. Dishonest, lazy and overpaid cretins."

"I make five dollars an hour."

"That's what I mean. Overpaid."

"Fuck yourself."

"I could call the law, you know."

"Call them."

"Jesus," she said, and started rolling the window up again.

Before she quite got it closed, I said, in a voice loud enough to attract the attention of several passersby, "There's at least a possibility that Mike Perry killed David Curtis, and you know it."

That was enough.

She stopped with the window. She looked as if somebody had kicked her in the stomach. She didn't even look quite so beautiful for a terrible moment there.

"Christ, I hope not," she said.

"We need to talk."

"I can't. Not right now. I'm late for an editing session."

"When's a good time then?"

"Tonight. Call me. I'm in the book."

"You think he did it, don't you?"

She shrugged. "He gets pretty jealous. He could have, I suppose. Or Hanratty."

"Hanratty?" That was totally unexpected. "Why Hanratty?"

"I'm not sure. I just know that several times over the past month David kept making all these dark suggestions about Hanratty."

"Like what?"

"Oh, like 'If we were smart, we wouldn't trust that asshole."

"You don't know what he was referring to?"

"No."

"I also need to talk to you about Stephen Chandler."

"The kid who killed himself?"

"Yes."

"Why?"

"His death may have something to do with Curtis's."

"Great," she said. Then she shook her head bitterly. "He

was a prick, that kid. He just wouldn't help us get the kind of interview we needed."

Her sentimentality was impressive.

"I'll call you tonight," I said.

"You don't really think he did it, do you?" she said.

"Who?"

"Mike Perry."

"I don't know."

"It would destroy his whole life. He'd never be able to work in the industry again."

Nice to know her values were in the right place.

"You ever want to own a tank?"

"Not that I can recall," I said.

"That's my ambition. Have my own tank."

"Well, we all have our dreams, I guess."

I was standing in the middle of the colosseum, where my casting agency had sent me for a week-long gig at the Guns and Ammo Exhibition. More than a thousand people milled around booths that housed every kind of weapon imaginable, except, of course, "your big military hardware," as Lynott, my boss here, had informed me. You want a hands-on look at your three-shot burst 9mm Beretta, you got it. You want to heft the Close Assault Weapon System (CAWS) with your full auto, Magazine-fed, optically sighted shotgun? Here you go. Or how about your Horton Safari Magnum crossbow for killers who don't like to make noise? Pick this little sucker up, bud.

And so on: Hermann Göring's wet dream.

Round and round the tight circle of booths they went, mostly suburban types, engineers, CPAs, ad-men, no different from farmers at a county fair examining produce and flowers, except that these guys were looking at hard-core weapons of death.

The tenor of the whole event was set by the huge poster that hung above the stage showing Sylvester Stallone in Rambo drag. In his headband and his shoulder-strap ammo belt and his carefully mussed hair, he looked like the Liberace of survivalists.

My part was pretty simple, actually. I'd been hired to don camouflage gear and grease my face and stand on the stage reading a lot of hokey copy provided me by Lynott, the guy who'd just asked if I'd ever wanted to own a tank.

"In this era, brave warriors must match their courage with the proper weaponry if freedom is to be preserved." Shit like that. In the old barn of a colosseum my voice bounced off the high ceilings and reverberated throughout the booths. Not that anybody paid attention. They were too orgasmically involved with guns.

"Part of learning your craft," as my agent always said. "An actor's got to take work where he can find it." Actually I was getting union scale, which worked out to be three times as much as my job for Federated Security paid.

"The hell of it is," Morg Lynott was explaining, "you can get the tank all right. It's getting the goddamn ammo that's the hard part. Leave it to the limp dicks in Washington to come up with a deal like that. They'll let you go out and buy your tank, but just try and buy ammo for the sucker and the firearms boys will be all over your ass like a rash."

Now you've already got him pictured as some good-old-boy slob who wants nothing more than to torture Democrats and homosexuals with bamboo shoots and electric prods, right? Wrong. And that's the hell of it. Morg Lynott is this big sheep dog of a man who runs a John Hancock insurance

72

agency and is actually a generous, warm and intelligent man. He just happens to be right wing and crazy as shit.

But that's a contradiction I've always found. Many of the neo-Nazi types I know are actually more decent human beings than many of the snotty liberals who polish their Volvos and give you big speeches about Civil Rights and The Bomb. When I'm around the do-gooders long enough, I also hate my humanitarian impulses.

"Yeah, that's a bitch, Morg," I said, "not being able to get ammo for your tank."

He laughed. "You're being a liberal again, Dwyer." He rubbed hands on his khaki jacket.

"I suppose I am."

"Nothing wrong with a guy having a tank. The Constitution gives us the right to bear arms."

"I suppose you're right. I've always wanted an aircraft carrier myself. You know, put it up there in my efficiency apartment, and I'd sleep a lot safer at night."

Then it was time to go back to the stage and read some more war stuff. Morg handed me the copy and said, "My wife wrote this stuff. We're damn proud of it."

I made the mistake of not reading it to myself first. Because when I got up there and actually started reading, I almost started laughing. The copy she wrote was about what would happen when the Russians invaded and saw all the beautiful American women. "If we aren't armed with our own auto pistols, with our own Enfield assault rifles, with our own mini-Uzi submachine guns, then these Russian bears are going to spread wide the unity of American virtue and drive deep into our very souls the thrusting rod of Communism."

Apparently, Mrs. Lynott read a lot of costume romances.

10

WHEN I CALLED MIKE PERRY'S PLACE, I WAS told by an answering machine that he could be found, if it was any kind of emergency, at the Windsor Park softball field.

The next place I checked was Federated Security to see if they wanted me to work tonight. Bobby Lee answered. "He told me to tell you you were put on suspension."

"Bullshit."

"Don't talk to me like that. I'm a lady."

"Right. And I'm an astronaut. Now let me talk to him."

There was a pause and then a shocking sound. She was crying. Bobby Lee with the beehive hairdo and the spandex pants was crying. In a soft voice—hell, her pain was pain even if I didn't like her—I said, "What's wrong, Bobby Lee?"

"He's taking her on vacation."

"Who?"

"His wife. That bitch."

So much for her being-a-lady theory.

"What's wrong with that?"

"He never takes me on vacation," she said.

"I see."

"You see what?"

"You're jealous."

"Well, that's a goddamn nice thing to say."

"It's perfectly understandable, Bobby Lee. I'd be jealous, too."

"You can just piss up a rope as far as I'm concerned."

Then she slammed the phone down.

There were a few dozen kids in wheelchairs lining a softball diamond. They were muscular dystrophy kids. They had twisted limbs and suffering eyes, and when they talked you could barely understand them. They just sat there and broke your fucking heart.

Next to the field knelt video-tape crews from two different TV stations recording the game itself.

On the mound was Mike Perry. He threw under hand the way Sonny Liston used to throw uppercuts. As if he were trying to penetrate a steel wall.

On first base was Bill Hanratty. While Perry did his pitcher routine—chomping Red Man, letting his fingers find just the right purchase on the rawhide, scratching his balls—Hanratty faced the bleachers and did what he did best: sang. He did "My Way" in his bad booming Irish voice, and all the housewives watching him loved it, clapping and pointing.

Now it would be easy to be cynical and say that Channel 3 and this CBS affiliate put on this softball game for MD kids just to get some self-serving footage on the six-o'clock news. And certainly that crossed their minds, I'm sure. But the charge of cynicism fell away when you looked at the kids themselves—their smiles and the way they moved excitedly in their wheelchairs. Nothing's pure: the stations were helping themselves, but you sure couldn't have proved it by the kids.

I sat in the stands for twenty minutes and enjoyed listening to the ball meet the bat and watching an over-weight news director make some spectacular catches out in right field. There were apple blossoms nearby, and an old guy with a battered tin box strapped around his shoulder sold hot dogs, and I said fuck it about nitrites and had me two of them, with as much mustard and onions as he could put on them.

After the game all the station personalities went up and spent time with the kids, and it was damn nice of them. The kids got even more excited. Dusk was coming, and the air was sweet with apple blossoms, and not too far away you could hear the river rushing, and close up there was the fragile laughter of these children, and at that moment the world seemed to be in pretty good shape.

Vans came up then, and the kids were put inside by a group of volunteer women. You had to marvel at these women—at their patience and love, in seemingly inexhaust-ible supply. Mike Perry and Bill Hanratty stood next to one of the vans and handed out autographed softballs. They kissed the little girls and patted the little boys on the backs. The vans left, headed down a winding asphalt road into a salmon-pink dusk.

From the trunks of cars came several cases of beer. The laughter on the air now was different, harsher, masculine. You could imagine that it would have sounded this way centuries earlier in the camps of Attila or Tiberius, just at dusk.

I came down from the bleachers, my hands still sticky from hot dogs, and went over and gave a guy a buck and took two Old Milwaukees from a cooler. Then I walked over to where Mike Perry and Bill Hanratty sat by the backstop. Hanratty recognized me first.

"Hey," he said.

"Hey," I replied.

By now Perry had recognized me. He scowled. I remembered how angry he'd gotten last night, blaming me for letting the killer into the building. But that was an unproved theory so far. The killer might easily have been inside the building. The killer might easily have been one of the Channel 3 newsteam.

"I wondered if I could talk to you," I said.

"What the fuck are you doing here?" Perry snapped.

"Asking questions."

"On whose authority?"

"Basically I'm trying to save my job," I said.

"I could give a rat's ass what you're trying to do," Perry said.

"C'mon. Let's at least give him a chance."

"He's some fucking security guard. Big deal."

"C'mon now, Mike. C'mon."

"Jesus," Perry said. He got up and hurled his beer into the backstop. Golden water sprayed everywhere. "Cocksucker," he said, and walked away.

It wasn't real difficult to imagine Mike Perry getting angry enough to kill somebody.

"Boy, he can really be a hothead."

"Yeah," I said.

"I don't know how the hell either one of us could help you, though. For one thing we're both still pretty much in shock. About Dave dying, I mean. Or being murdered, I guess you'd say."

"Yeah."

I just watched him as he talked. He had a fleshy handsome baby face, the world's most successful altar boy maybe, but watching him closely demonstrated to me that he was all artifice. It was in the eyes. The eyes did not reflect the words being spoken. No matter what he said, the eyes remained the same, hard and assessing. In my years on the force I'd noticed this trait in professional criminals: they needed certain social skills to be good at their trade—they had to hookwink everybody from their mates to their parole officers—and so they got very good at acting. Until you studied their eyes. Then they weren't worth a damn and they scared the shit out of you.

I decided to jab him hard. "Today somebody told me that David Curtis didn't trust you."

He had been drinking his beer. He stopped. Looked at me over the edge of the can. "What's that supposed to mean?"

"I don't have any idea."

"Then why ask me?"

"I wanted to see what you'd say."

"I guess now you know. I don't know what you're talking about."

"Do you know anybody who drives a black XKE?"

For the first time I had said something that caused some shift in his eyes. I had no idea what I was looking at. All I knew was that something had changed.

"No, I don't."

We stared at each other. After a while I said, "All right."

"Maybe I don't like this. Maybe Mike's right."

"About what?"

"About you. Why would you go around asking us questions? You're a security guard."

"I need to know what happened—otherwise I'm going to be blamed for letting the killer in, and I can't live with that. Besides, I need the job." I wasn't kidding him. I *was* going to be blamed, and I *did* need the job.

"Well, I've never said anything about blaming you, did I? It was that damn plumber."

"Did you know that Perry's girlfriend was sleeping with Curtis?"

He stared at me again. "Yes, I guess I did."

"You seem to be a pretty good friend of Perry's. How was he handling it?"

"Pretty good, I guess."

"Pretty good? Could you be a little more specific?"

"You mean do I think he killed Curtis?"

"Yeah, that's probably what I do mean."

"No, he didn't."

I watched his eyes closely again. "And you don't know anybody who drives a black XKE?"

He was a quick study. He'd been waiting for me. This time he said no and nothing changed in his gaze. Nothing at all.

I looked around. Perry was over in the bleachers.

"We brought separate cars," Hanratty said. "I guess I'll head back to the station."

I nodded.

"One thing," he said.

"What?"

He nodded over to the bleachers. "You fuck with him, he'll tear your face off. I've seen him when he gets angry."

"Yeah, I noticed that last night."

"That wasn't anything."

"You're not exactly helping his case. You should be trying to convince me what a sweet, gentle guy he is."

"He didn't kill Curtis. But he isn't any sweet, gentle guy, believe me."

"What about Curtis?"

"What about him?"

"Did you like him?" I asked.

"He was typical."

"Of what?"

"Of the people you meet in this business. We tend to worry about our careers to the exclusion of everything else. We put in very long hours and we don't get paid very well, all things considered, not on the local level anyway. So we tend to always be thinking about our careers and how we can improve them."

"Mind if I try my question again?"

"Did I like him, you mean?"

"Yeah."

"He was too much of a glamor boy for my taste. Kind of dark and good-looking and not much else. He wasn't what you'd call real deep."

"He did well with the ladies?"

"Very well."

"Anybody he was friendly with lately besides Marcie Grant?"

He frowned. "Kelly Ford."

I nodded. "You know anything about the Stephen Chandler story, the kid who committed suicide?"

"Just that it bothered Curtis a lot, when the kid died, I mean."

"He say anything to you about it?"

"He didn't have to. The day the kid died, Curtis went kind of crazy in one of the editing rooms. Damn near demolished the place."

"Guilt, maybe?"

"I suppose. I think he pushed those kids a little hard to get his story. Maybe he did blame himself."

The car starting in the gloom surprised me. Mike Perry was leaving.

"Guess you're going to have to catch him later," Hanratty said.

We shook hands.

"Thanks for talking," I said.

"I hope your job turns out all right."

I smiled. "So do I."

We went to our respective cars, got in and drove off.

I turned on the headlights. The spring night was chilly suddenly. I hit the heater. As we wound through the park, I felt snug with the Coltrane song on the jazz station and the womb of heat enveloping me. I just kept thinking about Hanratty's eyes. He was a much nicer guy than anybody else at the station and five times scarier.

Maybe that's why, as we drove between the birches that flanked the river, I decided to follow him.

By the time we reached the city, all the lights were on in the haze, red and yellow and blue neon against the gloom, the tall downtown buildings lit in the darkness. I had dropped back half a block. The easy way he drove told me that he didn't suspect I was behind him.

He led us within several blocks of the station, and by now I had no idea why I'd decided to tail him. Maybe I'd been bored and it had sounded like a way to deal with the monotony. But then he turned right when he should have turned left. He pulled into the parking lot of a sleazy motel that had a discreet little bar where couples who did not want to be seen could meet for drinks before going upstairs.

A tryst? Smiling Bill Hanratty, the happy altar boy who seemed to embody all the virtues middle America professes to love—a tryst?

He leaned against his car, watching people park and head inside. I was across the street, slouched down.

His body language told me he was nervous. He looked around too sharply and he couldn't stand still. He'd lean against his car and then he'd lean away from his car. He'd pace off a little circle and then he'd lean against his car again.

His anxiety was explained three minutes later, when another car pulled into the lot and he stalked over to it almost angrily.

The car was a black XKE.

11

FROM THERE THINGS HAPPENED QUICKLY.

Hanratty jumped into the black car and they were off. I hadn't gotten a single glimpse inside, because the windows were tinted nearly as black as the car itself.

A steady stream of traffic separated us. I waited with my ususal patience. Yelling and swearing at cars to hurry past. Slamming my fist on the dashboard a few times. Stomping my foot on the floor. Nobody seemed especially impressed. By the time I made my move, the XKE had disappeared out the back entrance of the motel.

I reached the parking lot, followed the course they must have taken and ended up at the entrance to a wide avenue filled with lovers strolling in the spring night and no sign of the black XKE.

Wonderful. I hadn't even had time to check out the license plate.

* * *

There were two black-and-whites and two unmarked cars parked in front of Falworthy House when I got there twenty minutes later.

The same kids I'd seen earlier in the day sat on the same stoop smoking cigarettes and spitting with practiced malice. When they saw me, the kids looked at each other and then back at me. Behind their easy contempt I now sensed something else.

"You the one who turned Mitch in?" the kid with the earrings said.

"No," I said.

"Well, somebody sure as fuck did."

Then I realized what I was hearing, and I don't know why it should have surprised me but it did. The kid was scared.

In back of them, Falworthy House loomed like a prison, front-yard lights angled to emphasize its institutional ambience. So many of its kids would graduate from here into real prisons and never know that there was another kind of life. Society had every right to protect itself from them, of course, but it had nothing to congratulate itself about, either. Nothing at all.

"He won't let them in."

"Who?" I asked.

"Mitch Tomlin. He's in the attic and he's got a shotgun."

"He's got this Remington," one of the other kids said in a kind of awe. "It'd put a hole in you this fucking big, man." He spread his hands wide to indicate the width of the damage it would do.

I went on up the stairs. Someone buzzed me in.

The place smelled of institutional food—meat loaf and green beans maybe—and disinfectant where the halls had been scrubbed down recently. In the vestibule I saw Karl Eler. He stood next to the staircase and shook his head over and over like one of those little dogs people put in the back windows of their cars. Across from him a hefty uniformed officer stood with his right hand resting on the handle of his Smith & Wesson.

"You with the press?" he asked me nervously. Obviously the press didn't know about this yet, and obviously nobody official wanted them to know.

Eler looked up and saw me. "My God," he said, "do you know what's happened?"

"One of the kids told me."

"Who is this guy?" the cop wanted to know.

"He's all right," Eler said. "He's trying to help Mitch. At least I think he is."

The cop frowned and walked a few steps away.

"When did this all happen?" I asked.

Eler went back to shaking his head. The life in him had begun to fade some time back—maybe about the time he realized that the sixties had failed its own dream or maybe about the time his wife had left him—and tonight was making it fade even faster. He was chalk white and his eyes were a washed-out blue. Even his flowered silk shirt and bell bottoms were faded from too many washings.

"Mitch got back here in time for supper, and I had a little talk with him about the things you and I discussed this morning," Eler said. "And he got very nervous. Obviously it was him you saw in Channel Three last night. Then he went upstairs to the attic and locked himself in. I got worried, so I called the police—I wanted to make sure we didn't have another Stephen Chandler incident on our hands—so when the officers started talking to him, they found out two things. One, that he had a shotgun with him, and two, that he was afraid he was going to be blamed for David Curtis's death last night."

"He told them he was in Channel Three?"

"Yes," Eler said. "Mitch is the confessional type, I'm afraid."

I could imagine a crimnal lawyer listening to our conversation. They always like to hear their clients are the confessional types.

A few girls came down a long hallway. They were crying. One of them, a short chunky blonde with a masculine haircut, came up and slid her arm around Eler, and he patted her much as you would a dog. "It'll be all right," he said, but there wasn't much conviction in his voice.

Then there was the gunshot, and it was so loud and unexpected that it had the impact of something supernatural on the moment. Eler's whole body jerked; I'm not sure what mine did.

The uniformed man in the vestibule said, "Holy Christ," and went running up the stairs a lot faster than his heft should have allowed him. The chunky girl whom Eler had been embracing backed away from him and slid over to the other two girls. They all held each other and gazed silently up the long stairs, at the top of which the shotgun blast still echoed.

I'd caught a domestic disturbance once where a steel-worker on a Friday night had put a twenty-two gauge to the temple of his three-year-old and inside the mouth of his faithless wife. Then he'd put it to his own temple. They were just meat and nothing more than meat by the time we got to them, and when you realize that—that in a very real way we are nothing more than meat—the way you look at life is never quite the same again. You've lost you philosophical cherry, I guess.

I was afraid I was going to see something like that now,

and for a moment I didn't know if I could handle it. I wasn't going to vomit or get hysterrical, I'd be sure not to do anything like that, but if Mitch Tomlin had put the gun to himself, it was going to stay with me a long time, like an illness you can't quite shake.

Eler looked at me wild-eyed and started up the stairs. I grabbed his elbow and brought him back.

"I have to know what's going on up there," he said. He was almost shrieking. You could see in the girls' eyes that this was the kind of reaction they'd expected from him. Disappointment fought with pity in their gaze.

"No, you don't," I said.

"But Mitch, he's—"

"Whatever's happened, the police will take care of it. The best thing we can do for them is stay right here and let them handle it. It's their job."

"But what if they're hurting him?"

That was something else he'd carried over from the sixties. His distrust of cops, which was all well and good until you remembered that he'd called them in the first place.

"They're not hurting him," I said. "They're probably trying to help him."

He came down the stairs first. They already had him handcuffed. In his T-shirt and Levi's and short blond hair and sensitive face, he might have been James Dean in a juvenile-delinquent movie circa 1956.

"Oh, God, Mitch," the chunky blonde cried, "you're all right!"

But he wasn't there anymore. Something had happened upstairs and he just wasn't there anymore. He was like a junkie twenty minutes after shooting up. Not there.

A bald homicide detective kept a beefy hand on Mitch

Tomlin's bicep. The detective stopped when he reached Eler. "We need to question him at the precinct, Mr. Eler. We don't know if any charges will be filed other than pertaining to the weapon he had upstairs."

"But what happened? The gunshot—"

The detective nodded to Mitch Tomlin. "Apparently, he thought about killing himself, then changed his mind at the last second. The weapon was fired, but only into the wall."

The detective nodded, then led his prisoner outside. The handcuffs made a metallic noise as Mitch Tomlin walked. His eyes hadn't made any kind of contact with anybody while the detective and Eler had talked. He was in shock. Other detectives came down from upstairs. I didn't recognize one of them.

I had come here to talk to Mitch Tomlin and Diane Beaufort about last night. Now that Tomlin was gone, I needed to find Beaufort. I wandered back to the kitchen and waited until Eler was free. The kitchen reminded me of the kind you see on military bases. Big and clean and well organized. There probably weren't a lot of great meals fixed here. Just big and clean and well-organized ones.

In ten minutes Eler came back. You could tell he was about to cry, and that didn't sound like so terrible an idea actually.

"I suppose they're just going to give up, aren't they?"

"What?" I asked.

"The police. I've always heard that."

He was babbling. "Heard what?"

"That they just decide who is the killer and slant their whole investigation to that. They don't even consider any other possibilities."

"A lot of what happens next depends on what Mitch tells them."

"Did you see his face?" The tears were back in his voice. I nodded.

"I'm afraid of what he'll tell them."

"Then what I'd suggest is getting a lawyer as quickly as you can."

"I've got a friend in the public offender's office."

"Call him then. Right away."

He seemed surprised. "You don't think he did it?"

"I don't know."

"Maybe you're a pretty decent guy after all."

"You'd better get to the damn phone."

"Yes. Of course. Good idea." He looked to be in shock himself.

"Where do I find Diane Beaufort?" I asked as he was going through the kitchen door.

He turned. Seeming confused again. "Probably, uh, at work."

"Where's work?"

"There's a Hardee's about four blocks from here."

"All right. Thanks."

He was back to shaking his head. "You really don't think he did it, do you?"

"He was there last night and he shouldn't have been. He was bitter over Stephen Chandler's suicide. If I were a homicide detective, I'd have to take a damn good look at him."

"My God," he said, "they're really going to charge him with murder, aren't they?"

Gently, I said, "You'd better get to the phone, Karl."

12

SHE HAD THE KIND OF UPTILTED NOSE AND WIDE eyes that fashion photographers go slightly crazy for. Her blond hair was pulled back in a bun, her blue eye makeup was applied a bit heavily, and she needed to lose maybe five pounds of baby fat—but in all, and even in her brown Hardee's uniform, Diane Beaufort was a classic beauty.

She was behind the counter, using one of those little metal chutes they fill french-fry bags with. I recognized her from last night. The tall kid with the baseball for an Adam's apple noticed me and stepped up instantly, perhaps fearing I was a Hardee's inspector.

"Help you?"

"I'd like to speak with Diane."

He looked back over his shoulder.

Diane was watching us. Frowning. Then she put down the french-fry device and wiped her hands with such elaborate care that all my cop instincts got riled.

"Hey, Diane," the kid said, as if she hadn't heard me.

She had, of course. Which was why she was taking off. In less than ten seconds she was gone.

I ran out the door, around the side of the big window where mommies and daddies sat feeding their kiddies. The air was sweet and gentle and made me feel young and needful of sex. Instead, I was running alongside a Hardee's window providing a few moments of TV-like entertainment for the diners watching me.

In the rear, big lights shone on an open area of dumpsters and empty egg crates. She wasn't there. I ran to one end of the parking lot. No sign of her. Nor had any car taken off. I ran west to a street shaded by blooming elm trees that cast peaceful shadows on the pavement. I squinted, peering as far down the street as I could see. Nothing. No sign of her whatsoever.

I went back to the Hardee's. The exhaust fans kicked everything in my direction. I felt as if I had been buried alive inside a hamburger.

There was only one other possibility.

I went in the back door. Down a corridor I could see the backs of several uniformed high school kids preparing various kinds of food. A radio played loud rock and roll. Nobody noticed me.

I went along the corridor until I came to two doors marked MEN and WOMEN. I had to wait five minutes before a female came along. She was a black girl, pretty in a gangly way, with amused but now suspicious eyes.

"I need you to do me a favor," I said.

"Nobody's supposed to be back here but employees." She looked around. I could picture a manager rushing out. I could picture a scene.

I took out my wallet. Showed her my Federated ID.

"This doesn't mean you're a policeman," she said.

"No, but it does mean that I'm a guy who's trying to do somebody a favor."

"Who?"

"Diane Beaufort."

"Diane's nice."

"I know. That's why I'm trying to help her."

"So what do you want me to do?"

"Go in the women's john and see if she's in there."

Her eyes, which had gotten friendly for a time, were suspicious again.

"Is she hiding from you?"

I had the take the chance of telling her the truth. "Yeah. But she doesn't know that I'm trying to help her."

"I'll bet."

"Just tell her this. Tell her that Mitch Tomlin was arrested tonight."

"Mitch Tomlin? The boy from Falworthy?"

"Yeah."

"God."

"Please tell her."

She stared at me a moment then nodded. "Okay."

She was gone two or three minutes. In the interim a boy in a brown uniform walked past me and said, "You're not supposed to be back here."

"I know."

Then he just kept walking right out the back door.

The girl led Diane Beaufort out a few minutes later. "He has a badge," the girl said, "but it doesn't mean anything." Diane nodded. She stood straight and still, as if she were about to be executed. The girl said, "You want me to wait with you?"

Diane shook her head.

The girl looked at Diane and then looked at me and left.

"How about going out in the parking lot?" I said. "It's sort of tough to talk in here." And it was: too narrow, too shadowy, with people hovering on the edges.

"No," she said.

"The police arrested Mitch tonight."

"That's what Loretta said."

"Do you think he killed David Curtis?"

"No."

"Don't you want to help him?"

"Yes."

After a few zombie-like exchanges I finally realized I was dealing with a very stoned young lady.

"Can you take some time off?"

"When?" she asked.

"Right now."

"I don't know."

"You need to get straight."

She touched nail-bitten fingers to a beautiful cheekbone. "I know. I'm pretty fucked up."

"What would help?"

"Probably walking around. There's a place down by the river."

"Fine."

"You're not going to hustle me or anything?"

"No."

"You promise?"

"I promise," I said.

"I'll bet he's scared."

"Who?"

"Mitch."

"Yeah."

"Mitch isn't real tough. That's why I was surprised he had guts enough to go to Channel Three last night."

"Why were you there?"

"When I figured out where he'd gone, I just wanted to go and see if he was all right and everything."

For a time neither of us said anything. Just listened to birds in the trees, to the last bell at St. Michael's for the day.

"I got some tapes," she said.

I wanted to get going, but she was so precariously stoned that I didn't want to alarm her by pushing too hard and too fast.

"What kind of tapes?"

"Of when Stephen was being interviewed about suicide."

"When he was on TV, you mean?"

She nodded.

"Maybe you'd let me borrow them," I said.

"If you promise to bring them back."

"All right." I put out my hand and touched her on the shoulder. "You need to walk around," I said.

Maybe because we're so landlocked out here, maybe that's why the river plays so important a role in this city. You see people walking the shoreline even when it's cold enough to wear a winter jacket.

We sat on a park bench that needed to be painted for the new season and looked at a speedboat perform some stunts until the police patrol boat showed up, all harsh white lights and bullhorns, and forced the guy out of the water. There was a good possibility the guy was drunk.

I had bought two big containers of coffee and, at her

94

request, a pack of Winston Lights. She smoked and bit her nails and looked beautiful in a forlorn way.

"Curtis definitely killed him," she said.

"Killed Stephen Chandler, you mean?"

"Yeah, and when you see the tape you'll know what I'm talking about. He really forced him to—to talk about things Stephen didn't want to."

"Like what?"

"Like about getting somebody pregnant and stuff and not being able to handle it."

"Stephen had gotten somebody pregnant?"

"Yes," she said. "Me."

I just watched her.

"Then Curtis kept pushing him to talk about his old man and how his old man committed suicide."

"Stephen's father committed suicide?"

"Yeah. He was in prison and he just couldn't take it anymore. So one day he drank some bleach and died."

"Why was he in prison?"

"Killed a guy who'd been sleeping with Stephen's mother."

"I see."

"Kind of low rent. That's what Stephen always called it. 'Low rent.' He was always real ashamed about it. But it was my fault Curtis asked him about it."

"Your fault?"

"Umm-hmm. Curtis talked to me about Stephen. You know, about how Stephen had tried to kill himself three times in the year before he did the interview. I also told him about Stephen's father."

I nodded. Now I was curious about the tapes. "I guess I never understood the circumstances of Stephen's death. How did he die?"

"OD'd."

"On what?"

"Smack."

"How long had he been doing heroin?"

"Maybe six months. He started when he started hanging around the apartment."

"What apartment?" I asked.

"Downtown."

"Whose apartment is it?"

"I'm not sure."

"You're losing me, Diane." Her vagueness was starting to make me irritable. "Please tell me about the apartment, okay?"

"You getting pissed?"

"No, it's just my old man's crankiness."

She didn't laugh, of course, because for someone as young as she was, there was no irony in my line. I was indeed, for her, an old man.

"So how about the apartment?" I said.

"Stephen met these guys a while back."

"What guys?"

"These twins."

"They have names?" The irritation was back in my voice.

"John and Rick."

"Last name?"

"I'm not sure. But they're the reason we broke up, me'n Steve. John and Rick were 'the good life,' as Steve always said. I guess I wasn't. He had money, clothes all of a sudden."

"What happened when you got pregnant?"

"We found this woman."

96

"You mean an abortion?"

"Yeah. This woman. Anyway it didn't take very long. I think it bothered Steve more than me. He got really fucked up on reds and wine that night and started hitting stuff, you know, pounding his fist into stuff, and he ended up breaking two of his knuckles."

"What about John and Rick? What do they do?"

"Have a lot of money. That's all I know."

"Can you tell me how to get to their apartment?"

"Sure." She described the place. It was an expensive high-rise building west of a large city park.

"How long did Stephen know them?"

"I'm not sure. Not exactly. He only started talking about them a few months before he died."

"Didn't Karl Eler know Steve had become a junkie?"

She laughed unpleasantly. "Karl's a nice guy, but he should have been a minister. That's why his old lady up and split. She couldn't take all his sermons. Anyway, Eler wouldn't know enough to see that somebody was a junkie, not unless they shot up right in front of him. He's real naive."

For now I'd learned enough. Junkies and walking-out wives and men in prison who drank bleach and teenagers who kept trying to kill themselves until they got it done. Sometimes your mind can contain only so much. What's the Bob Dylan line? *I need a dump truck, Mama, to unload my head.* I know what he means.

So for a time I just sat and watched the river and tried to imagine what the shores must have looked like in my great-grandfather's day. There were barges then, headed for the Mississippi, and nearby there had been a dock where kids came to watch the boats. I had seen ink sketches of it all in an old book. The kids in the sketches were immortal, grinning and waving as they would always grin and wave, and the boatmen waved back for all time, too. There had never been a time like that, of course, not really, the human lot being what it is, but it was nice to think otherwise, nice to think that teenage girls hadn't always been the shambles that Diane Beaufort was.

"He was trying to quit," she said after a time.

"Stephen?"

"Yes."

"How do you know?"

"A few nights before he died, he snuck into my room— Eler doesn't want boys and girls in the same room, you know—and he started crying and he told me. He said he'd gone for four days and was going to turn himself into this rehab center."

"You think he was serious?"

"I know he was."

"How?"

"He asked me to meet him at this church the next day. I did. We went up to the rail, you know in front of the altar, and we said prayers together. I thought, Whoa, he's really serious about this."

"Did he actually go to the center?"

"I think so."

"But you're not sure?"

"Not positive."

"May I have the name of the center?"

"Sure. The Stillman Center."

I knew where it was. I watched the river some more but the images of the waving kids and the barges were gone. Now I smelled the factories downriver and watched a

13 I HAD DINNER AT A DENNY'S. UNLIKE THE other chains, it serves something remotely resembling food. While I ate, I watched the other diners. Mostly couples. When you're alone as much of the time as I am, you get resentful of couples. How happy and safe and secure they look. After I finished my meal, I got a mint and a toothpick to keep the feast going, and then I found a pay-phone and got hold of Edelman.

"Tonight a kid named Mitch Tomlin was arrested," I said.

"He's a nice kid. They called me after class and I stopped down. I listened to him answer questions through the glass. He's a nice kid and I hate to see him get nailed for it."

"He didn't do it."

He laughed. "I'm glad you've got your old confidence back."

"I'm serious." Then I explained, as I had explained last night, how Tomlin's muddy prints tracked down the stairs but stopped long before he could have reached David Curtis's dressing room.

"You ever think that the cyanide was put into the laxative somewhere other than at the station?"

"No."

"Well, you should. And you should also consider each member of the newsteam a suspect. They have plenty of motives for wanting him dead."

"I would, but something's come up to change my mind."

"What?"

"Mitch Tomlin's confession."

"You're kidding."

"I'm not. They got a confession out of him."

"I know why he's saying it."

"You mean you don't believe him?"

"No," I said, "I don't. He's trying to avenge his friend's death. Or he's trying to protect somebody."

"Who?"

I thought of Diane Beaufort and her miserable relationship with Stephen Chandler that ended with two guys named John and Rick and an abortion. Diane had been at Channel 3 last night.

"You got a better suspect in mind?"

"No," I said, wanting to change the subject. No point in getting Diane involved when I didn't need to.

"But you still don't think he did it?"

"No I don't."

"A confession's pretty hard to deny."

"He's probably a doper. You know how fucked up they get."

He sighed. "I'm afraid you're not convincing me."

"That doesn't mean I'm going to stop trying."

This time his laugh was not happy. "I didn't figure you would." He coughed and said, "You like playing cop again?"

"Not really. I'm seeing all the same bullshit that drove me away."

"I know what you mean. You get squared around with Becker?"

"Seems there isn't anything for me to do tonight for Federated."

"He came over last night after you left and talked to Robert Fitzgerald. The way he was browning up to him, I was afraid of what he was going to do right there in public."

"There's another beauty."

"Fitzgerald?"

"Yes. When you look at his gimp leg you want to feel sorry for him, but then you look at his face, at his arrogance, and you think, Fuck you, buddy."

"He's even worse when he's hysterical."

"I can imagine."

"We've got our killer, Dwyer."

"You back on that?"

"Yeah. The kid did it, the Tomlin kid."

"C'mon, Edelman. It's too easy."

"A confession is easy?"

"Take care of yourself," I said.

"You hanging up?"

"Yeah."

"You asshole."

"Thanks."

I hung up.

I found another quarter and tried Marcie Grant. I'd promised to call her. I was still curious about Mike Perry's relationship with Curtis. The sportscaster sounded jealous of Curtis—one of the three best reasons, according to police stats, to kill somebody. Her line was busy. I wrote down her address.

The Brenton Arms was the first condo high rise in the city, and as such it had attracted all the very wealthiest people in the first few years of its existence. Its imitators were for the less wealthy and less prestigious. As if to prove my point, there was even a stretch limo parked in front of the lobby tonight. In the darkness the Brenton towered far up above the blossoming apple trees. I got past the first glass door all right, but not into the lobby. For that you needed a special coded card.

A white-haired couple who looked like a retirement ad were in the process of inserting their own special card. I knew I didn't have a chance of getting inside. I'd have to ask my questions out here. I showed them my Federated ID.

The man said, "You're not a policeman."

"No, I'm not."

"Then why are you bothering us?"

"I just need some information."

"Would you move your foot please?"

"Sure."

The door closed and they rode up.

Five minutes later I stood in front of the inner door and looked out at the city. An ambulance went by, then a squad car. Teenagers drove by, apparently poor ones, because when they got abreast of the Brenton a kid with a mean face stuck his head out and gave the entire apartment building and all its inhabitants the bird.

"May I help you with something?"

He was as old as the man and woman who'd gone up in the elevator, but where they were fresh, he was weary. He was black and he had obviously spent his life paying the penalty for it.

He came over in a new gray uniform, a big mop filling his hands. My father'd had such a job, cleaning up buildings after hours. A second job. My father had made the mistake of having too many kids. My mother hadn't exactly lived like a queen, either.

When I showed him the Federated piece, he looked at it very hard with his whipped brown gaze and said, "I don't want no trouble, sir."

His "sir" embarrassed me. "There are twins who live here. Men. John and Rick."

"Yessir." He gripped his mop handle tightly, as if it were a lifeline.

"I'd like to talk to them."

"I don't believe they're home, sir."

"Would you mind giving me their name?"

He looked at me, paused. "I guess that wouldn't hurt none."

I took out my nickel pad. Tried to make it look official.

"Ayres is their name. Ayres."

"Anything you can tell me about them?"

He shook his head. "Nothing I better say, sir."

I glanced around the empty lobby. "Doesn't seem there's anybody around to listen."

"No, sir, I guess not."

I reached in my pocket. I had three crumpled ones and some change that counted out to three quarters and two dimes and a penny. I'd never tried to bribe anybody before.

I wasn't sure you could do it with three singles and three quarters and two dimes and a penny.

He watched me figure out my change. A gentle smile played at his lips. I must have looked like a fucking bozo trying to play private eye with a routine like this.

"How would you like three dollars and ninety-six cents?"

"Like in the movies?" Now his smile was more apparent.

"What the fuck," I said, "you could buy a six-pack or something."

He leaned on his mop some more. "You must be new at this."

"Well," I said, sounding defensive.

He shrugged. "Ain't much I could tell you anyway other than that they're kind of strange. Real into body building and flying in and out of the city all the time. They must make four, five trips a week."

"What do they do for a living?"

"Ain't sure. Heard them tell a fellow once that they sold men's clothes. They might, too, the way they dress. Real fancy dudes." He smiled with pink gums and bad teeth and the first dim light of pleasure in his eyes. "They got enough women, I'll say that for them."

"You ever see a teenage boy hanging around them?"

He shrugged. "Saw several."

I described Stephen Chandler. "You ever seen him?"

He thought for a time. "Yes, sure. He was around here."

"Why do you think these boys hung around?"

He smiled again. "Oh, I know why they hung around. They'd do errands for the twins and the twins would let them stay in the condo. Booze, women, whatever they wanted. Guess they even got some of them porno movies up there."

A fuzzy picture was beginning to emerge and I felt sorry as hell for Stephen Chandler.

"You don't think they're home?"

"No, sir."

We were back to that.

"If I gave you a number to call would you call it when they come back?"

"I get off in five more hours."

"Well, if they come back during that time, would you give me a call?"

"Yes, sir, I guess I would. Yes, sir."

I wrote the number down and handed it to him. He nodded and put it into the pocket of his gray work shirt. I took the money I'd been holding in my own shit pocket and handed it over to him.

"You don't need to do that," he said.

"You should get something out of this," I said.

"Well, I guess I could buy me a sixer or something."

I gave him the money.

14 MARCIE GRANT SURPRISED ME BY LIVING IN A trailer court. New as the mobile homes were, tidy as the landscaping was, it still had that mazelike aspect that reminded me of a prison camp. It all seemed wrong for a young beautiful blonde with stunning violet contacts.

Lights shone erratically in a handful of trailers as I drove down the moonlit lanes looking for 4017. I recognized her car and the car parked next to hers at an angle, as if the driver had slammed to a halt and jumped out before the engine had quite shut off. The car was the one Mike Perry had driven away in this afternoon in order to avoid talking to me.

I killed my lights, parked and got out. The breeze was so spring sweet and the sky so clean, I just wanted to stand here, not know a damn thing more about any of these people, just stand here and forget it all. A pontifical Alan Alda speech on a "M*A*S*H" rerun coming from a nearby trailer brought me back to dour reality. I looked around, made as sure as I could that nobody was watching me, then went along the side of Marcie Grant's trailer to the rear window. I tried not to think of the charge I'd be facing if I got caught. I didn't even know why the hell I was doing this.

The skin of the trailer was silver and shone in the moonlight. Alongside the west end of it ran a hopeful little garden that the local dogs probably used as a toilet. The back window was high enough for me to have to stand on my tiptoes and lean over, not wanting to step on her garden, for a look inside.

The bed was mussed, blankets hanging off the edge and dragging on the floor, and clothes were strewn every place imaginable. One exceptional touch was a pair of panties hanging on a doorknob. Marcie Grant had obviously graduated from the same housekeeping school I had.

I tried to swallow my next few breaths so I could hear better. Alan was still pontificating, but when I listened just below his level, I heard something terrible. Weeping.

Ducking down, I moved around the rear of the trailer to the other side. The first thing I checked out was the trailer facing Marcie's. The windows were all dark. I proceeded along the east side then until I reached a window halfway down, where a light burned.

Mike Perry stood naked to the waist, a can of Pabst in one big hand, looking down at Marcie Grant. His chest was expansive and hairy, but that wasn't what mattered at all. What mattered was the fist he held—almost as if it didn't belong to him—the fist that shone with blood.

Marcie was crouched on the couch, holding her hands over her mouth, blood seeping out between the fingers.

He had hit her and hit her hard.

"You fucking bitch," he said.

"I'm sorry, I shouldn't have told him, I'm sorry." When she talked, she sounded as if she'd just gotten novacaine.

"You should've heard what he said to me, that faggot."

Perry should have sounded angry. Instead he sounded oddly hurt, as if she'd been the one who'd struck him. " 'Can't take care of your women anymore, so I thought I'd help you out.' " Perry smashed his beer into the wall. He lunged at her and jerked her to her feet and slapped her once very precisely across the mouth.

I reacted instinctively. I moved around the front of the trailer and got to the door and jerked on the handle. It surprised me by opening. Perry, who had maybe five inches in height and forty pounds in weight on me, filled the doorway.

"What the fuck are you doing here?" he said. He was angry, which had increased his strength considerably. He reached down like a monster in a Japanese movie and plucked me off my feet and jerked me up the three steps and inside.

It was like being in a car wreck, everything spinning around so quickly, my mind feeling completely out of control. I couldn't even get in a good punch. Not that I thought it would do a lot of good anyway. He threw me down in the approximate vicinity of Marcie Grant. My elbow caught her in the arm, and she groaned.

"You sonofabitch, what the hell're you doing here?" He was a berserk animal, and I saw then that he was drunk enough and angry enough for no amount of reasonable talking to help. So much for the psych courses they made you take in police school.

What I did next had nothing to do with bravery—only simple survival. If I didn't do something, he'd keep me pinned down here all night and bash my head in at will. I eased up off the couch, and just as he came for me, I kicked a perfect Super Bowl field goal, one that just happened to catch him high and hard in the balls.

He went down with a look of agony on his face and a bellow of confusion and rage tearing open his mouth.

The next one landed just below his temple, and this time he went out instantly. He pulled a table lamp down with him. When it hit the floor, brilliant light splashed in every direction, like a strobe.

I went over and stood by him a few moments, just making sure.

"Is he all right?" Marcie said, sounding a little hysterical.

I knelt down, knees cracking, and felt for a pulse. "Yeah," I said, and stood up.

"You sure don't believe in fighting fair, do you?"

"I don't fight to make friends. I fight to save my ass."

"Jesus," she said, looking down at Perry and shaking her head.

I looked around the trailer. "You have any beer?"

She flung a left hand toward the refrigerator. The other hand she kept pressed against her mouth.

I found the Pabst and opened one and said, "Why was he beating you up?"

She shrugged. She wore men's cotton pajamas and looked as ravishing as a young Rita Hayworth. Not even the blood spoiled the effect. "I told somebody something about him that I shouldn't have."

"I need to know what you said and who you said it to."

"Fuck off," she said. "You're some goddamn security guard. Big deal." She fussed with her mouth some more. "Anyway, they got the kid who killed Curtis. It's all over."

"The kid didn't do it. One of you did it."

"One of who?"

"One of you at the station."

"Killed Curtis?"

"Yeah."

113

"How do you know? You're just some loser playing cop."

"Why was Perry so angry tonight?"

"You're the one who knocked him out. Why don't you wake him up and ask him?"

"I want to know from you."

Just then Perry moaned, and the way she jumped I saw how deep her fear of him ran. For just an instant her practiced tough veneer faded and she looked young and frightened.

"You need a friend," I said.

She watched him—he looked like a felled mastodon there on her floor—and faintly she said, "Yeah."

She wouldn't let me help her. She spent twenty minutes in the john getting her mouth cleaned up. I sat by the open window watching the clouds race the moon. By now Perry was snoring.

She came out in fresh pajamas with her hair pulled back. She made instant coffee in a microwave and brought two big mugs over.

"You feel like talking?" I said.

"Why not?" She sounded almost bitter. "You want to know why Michael was so mad tonight, right?"

"Right."

"You really don't think that kid did it?"

"No."

"You think one of us did it?"

"Yeah."

"Michael?"

"Maybe."

"Shit. I'm really going to sound like a terrible person when I say this."

I just waited for her to say it. She had to work up the nerve.

"I started seeing David Curtis on the side. And one night when I was pretty drunk, I told him about Michael's problem."

I still waited. She was just getting going.

"About his sexual problem, I mean. Most of the time, Michael's impotent. It's especially tough for him. I mean here's this big NFL player, this really handsome guy that all the women think is so neat, and most of the time he has trouble in bed. Not all the time, sometimes he's just fine and it's really great, but sometimes . . ." She shook her head. Stared down into her coffee cup, then over at Perry.

"For the past seven months we've been seeing a counselor," she went on. "He charges us seventy dollars an hour to say the same thing over and over. Michael doesn't trust women and that's why he has this problem. He beats me up sometimes, like tonight, especially when he's drinking. Most of the time I try to accept it and I don't blame myself, but I get in moods and— It's not even that I get horny or anything, but sometimes I just need to be with somebody where it's uncomplicated, where you can just have fun, you know? That's why I was with David Curtis. It was very uncomplicated until I got drunk one night and told him, and— Well, that changed our relationship, mine and David's. He started making jokes about Michael. 'The little prick that couldn't.' Juvenile stuff like that. David was a pretty boy and he'd always been intimidated by Michael, because he was so much bigger and stronger. Then one night when we were all drunk at a bar, David said something to Michael, and Michael knew that not only had I been sleeping with other men but that I'd told his secret. You can see what it did to him."

I couldn't help myself. While I didn't have any regrets

about kicking him, I felt sorry for him now. He was a victim. "You've just given Perry a strong motive for killing Curtis," I said.

"I know. That's why I didn't want to say anything."

"You've given yourself a reasonably strong motive, too."

"Me? Why?"

"Revenge. In a way he betrayed you. By making jokes about something you'd confided seriously to him."

"I guess he did betray me."

"I don't get the impression from anybody that he was exactly a wonderful guy."

"He wasn't. He was an airhead with the right looks and the right style. He never would have been major—I mean he was too stupid to make it at the networks."

I finished my coffee. "Do you know anything about a break-in at Kelly Ford's office?"

"Just that it made Kelly very nervous. It would make me nervous, too."

"What do you think of her?"

She frowned slightly. "If I say what I feel, then I'll just sound catty."

"Say it."

"She's very bright and very nice, but she's really kind of mixed up. She left a husband and two children to go out into the world and prove herself, but now she's fallen into the worst chauvinist trap of all. She's somebody's mistress."

"Robert Fitzgerald's?"

"Right, She's—silly about him. Like a teenage girl. If he's angry with her, she just goes to pieces. You know?"

"I know."

"And he's been in a pretty bad mood lately."

"Know why?"

"Sure. He's made some extremely bad investments that have depleted his cash flow, and our ratings keep going down. He's in big trouble—there are even rumors he's going to be forced to sell the station. And for him that's going to be a real blow. He never finished college. Instead—this was back in the early sixties, I guess—he was a grip at Channel Three. Reigers, the guy who originally owned it, really admired Fitzgerald and sort of adopted him. He was impressed that anybody who had a lame leg and had come from such an impoverished background would have the drive that Fitzgerald did. Eventually, by the time Reigers died, he had made it possible for Fitzgerald to own the station. If Fitzgerald had to sell it now, he would lose face—and his pride is incredible. He's been taking his troubles out on everybody, but especially on Kelly."

"Do you like her?"

"I feel sorry for her. I don't think that's the same thing."

I stood up. Perry groaned again. "What happens when he wakes up?"

She glanced down at Perry again. Shook her head. "I'm afraid to find out. The last few days he's changed, he's . . ." She shook her lovely hair. "He's even more violent . . ."

"I'll take him with me if you want."

"That would just make things worse."

"You sure?"

"I'm sure."

Then she touched her fingers to her mouth. "Damn," she said.

"What?"

"It's bleeding again."

15

TWENTY MINUTES LATER I WAS ON AN EMPTY one-way street that ran along the river. The water smelled clear and cold. The moon was huge and red, hanging just behind a line of pine trees. I had the radio up loud. I wanted to be younger and smarter. I wanted my kid to be three again and safe on my knee. I wanted to do all the things I had failed to do properly in my life. That's a special kind of hell.

I drove till the street became a two-way headed out into the country, and then I turned around and came back into the city. I had a bad idea. But at least it was an idea. I found a phone booth and a phone book and looked up Kelly Ford's address.

Young people with money had been through her neighborhood recently. Five years ago the massive old homes that sat along this avenue had been home to the nomadic poor. Then the Volvos moved in. The homes had been restored to the splendor they'd enjoyed back when big black Packards had been the measure of prestige. Her apartment house came complete with turrets and a captain's walk. It was three stories high and had a front porch wide enough to play touch football on. Inside the vestibule were six mailboxes, each with its own intercom. I pressed hers. She surprised me by answering immediately. It was after midnight.

"Yes?"

"It's Dwyer."

"Jack?"

"Yes."

"Is everything all right?"

"I'm just in kind of a weird mood, I guess." It was one of those enigmatic and maybe even meaningless statements that make a lot of sense to people as neurotic as myself.

"Come on up."

I was as idiotically happy as a freshman who'd just gotten his first date.

She lived on the top floor. From her hallway window you could look down through the tops of blooming elms at the shadows the leaves played on the street. It was beautiful. It made me want the night never to end.

"We must have some kind of telepathy," she said as soon as she opened the door. She smiled her electric smile. "I'm in a weird mood myself."

She was wearing a very formal blue robe that fit her with the grace of an evening gown. Even without makeup she still looked lovely. She carried herself with an easy grace that fascinated me.

Her apartment resembled something you'd see in a decorator magazine. Plants of every description filled the place. The art prints ran to modernist, especially Chagall. The furnishings were modern, too, but cushiony enough to be comfortable. Low on the stereo I recognized Handel. The titles in her bookcase were mostly psychology and studies of media. Not a scrap of poetry, not even a cheap but amusing novel. I wasn't sure why, but I was disappointed.

"Would you like some tea?"

"You wouldn't have a beer, would you?"

"I'm afraid I don't drink beer."

"Okay. Some tea. That sounds fine."

She laughed. "You don't sound like it sounds fine. I have wine."

"Wine would be great."

She nodded to the bookcase. "I couldn't help but notice you looking at my books. You didn't pick one of them up."

"I guess I like novels."

"I used to, but at my age I'm afraid I don't have time for novels. Too much to learn too fast."

At the mention of her age a certain bitterness had come into her voice, and I wondered why. I was obviously here on a mission straight from my loins. Her age didn't bother me any. Before I could respond, she said, "I'll get your wine," and left the room.

Near the window inside an otherwise empty bookcase were photographs of a handsome if rather pompous-looking man her age and three very attractive children, two college-age girls and a boy who looked as if he might be athletic.

I was studying them all more closely when she came back adn handed me my wine and said, "My family."

"Great-looking people."

"Yes, yes they are. And fortunately they're all doing well. Even Ken."

"Your husband?"

She nodded. "It took him several years to forgive me. I

think he has now. And now that he has forgiven me, there's no pain for him anymore. I think he's even got a woman friend."

"How about you?" I said. I thought of what Marcie Grant had told me about how she'd given up her family. "Are you over your pain?" I was also thinking about the scene this afternoon with Robert Fitzgerald. The air of masochism when she'd fled the restaurant.

"Do you mind if I ask you a question?"

"I guess not. I mean since you're not going to answer the question I asked you." I tried to make my statement wry. It just came out stupid.

"Why did you come up here tonight?"

"I've still got questions about the case."

I sensed panic in her and didn't have the faintest idea why. "They arrested that boy tonight. Tomlin."

"I heard. But he didn't do it."

"Are you serious?"

"Yes."

My mind kept playing back to her mood over the intercom. She'd been almost girlish at the prospect of seeing me. Now she was anxious, almost angry.

"I want to tell you something."

"All right," I said.

"For the past five years I've been Robert Fitzgerald's mistress."

I didn't know what to say. "I see."

"And what's even worse, I've been totally faithful. Totally."

This time I said nothing, just listened to the traffic on the street below, watched the play of shadows from the trees against the windows. You could almost hear the ghosts of a hundred years of conversations in this old room. Someday the two of us would be dead and ghosts trapped here, too. I needed sex rather desperately at that moment, not so much for itself, of course, but for the freedom from my burdens. Watching her so graceful in her robe, so arch and sad in one way and yet so vital and fresh in another, I went a little crazy from my need. I would have to get out of here. Fast.

"I just wanted you to know that, that I've been his mistress," she said, "and that I've been faithful and that right now I'm very frightened."

Then she reached out with slender, graceful fingers and brought my face gently to hers and I went genuinely crazy.

There was going to be a price for this kind of comfort, of course.

Just after my divorce I started dating an actress who'd been rather spectacularly dumped by a local dreamboat. There was a desperate edge to her lovemaking that made it thrilling for me, but afterward the desperation translated into something else entirely—her need to review and re-review what seemed like every single moment of their relationship. For the price of very pleasurable sex, I became her shrink. When she had told me everything she could possibly tell me, and when I had given her every peice of fatherly/brotherly/loverly advice I was capable of, she dumped me in a rather spectacular way and found a brand-new sympathetic set of balls and ears.

Kelly Ford had a little round belly, and her flesh was not a young woman's flesh, as mine was not a young man's flesh, but she was by turns clever and tender, and she tasted clean and wonderful, and her fingers were marvels and once, as I was kissing her breasts, I looked up and saw her eyes shine with something beautiful and unknowable and profoundly female.

Almost immediately afterward she started crying. "Damn him," she said and got up and went into the bathroom and stayed there for maybe fifteen minutes. Water ran and the toilet flushed and the medicine cabinet opened and closed and all I could do was lie on her bed and feel the physical relief that I floated on, almost like a marijuana high, and then the terrible sense, not unlike Kelly Ford's own I suppose, that I was in bed with the wrong person. I was starting to think about Donna Harris again and how much I missed her lopsided smile and what a shit I thought she was sometimes and how much I loved her anyway.

Kelly Ford came back and stook by the window. Against the moving patterns of streetlight and leaves she looked lovely and dramatic.

"I really enjoyed myself," she said. She sniffled tears.

"Yes. And you sound like it, too."

Her laugh was gorgeous. "I'm sorry I just got up and left. I got overwhelmed, I guess."

"I understand."

"That's the nice thing about you. I think you do understand."

"I'm going through it myself."

"What?"

"An uncertain love affair."

"Is she married?"

"She's worse than married. She's divorced but she can't break the ties."

"Sounds terrible."

"It is."

"How long will you let it go like this?"

"How long have you let Robert Fitzgerald go like this?"

Her laugh again. This time tinged with a touch of anger. "I was hoping you'd say something brave and inspire me."

"The hell of it is, nobody can inspire you but you."

"I know. I've bored all my friends with my story so many times. And I've been to every kind of shrink there is. But— still."

"Yeah—still."

She turned away from the window, came back and sat down on the edge of the bed. It squeaked faintly and pleasantly in the deep shadows.

An image of teenaged Mitch Tomlin in the county lockup came to me. I didn't think he belonged there. I had to do something about it. I had to restore my own credibility as well. At least to myself.

"He's in trouble, isn't he?"

"Who?"

"Fitzgerald," I said.

"Who told you that?" It was a very sharp question, given that her room was still scented with our lovemaking.

"It doesn't matter. I'm working on a murder investigation, and there are things I need to know."

She touched my hand. "I'm sorry. I'm very defensive about him. Not many people like him, you know. Which seems to bring out my maternal feelings."

"I'm told he may have to sell the station."

She sighed. "Yes. That's one possibility that's come up."

I decided to ask her straight out. "Would he have any reason to kill David Curtis?"

"I knew that's what you were leading up to."

"You're getting defensive again."

She got up and went over to the window. She wore a half

slip, and in the leaf-shifting light her small stomach might have been a young girl's in the early stages of pregnancy. Her shoulders sagged. This was not good for her, and I felt like hell but I had to think of the job.

"He didn't kill him."

"You're sure of that?" I asked.

"He had no reason to."

"Maybe there's something you don't know."

"There's nothing I don't know about Robert Fitzgerald."

"You don't sound completely happy about that."

"I'm not. In fact it irritates me. He spends his nights here confiding all his troubles to me, and he always leaves saying, 'You've made me feel much better. Thank you.' Then he goes home to his wife. She gets him when he's feeling good about himself."

I thought of Bobby Lee and her jealousy over the fact that Becker was taking his wife on vacation. Being a mistress isn't easy.

"Do you have the tapes of the Chandler boy?"

"The series we did on suicide you mean?"

"Yes."

She nodded. "I keep duplicates of every special feature series we run back in my main office. Sometimes I study them, try to see what we did wrong or right."

"I was wondering," I said, "if I could see them."

"Sure. But why?"

"I'm not sure why. I just have a sense that they'd help me."

"I've got them in my office."

"Maybe I could stop by tomorrow."

"Of course."

"Around eleven or so."

"That would be fine." She still sounded troubled. "He's a decent man, you know. He's had a very tough life."

"I sensed that in him."

"Are you being sarcastic?"

"Jesus," I said, her defensiveness beginning to irritate me, "no, I'm not being sarcastic. All right?"

"I'm sorry. I really do like you a lot, and I'm afraid I'm fucking up our whole evening, aren't I?"

I calmed down. "All right."

"When he was six he was playing in a train yard. Just the thing mothers spend years telling their children not to do. Anyway, he tripped and a train came along and—" Her bare shoulders shuddered. Inwardly I shuddered a bit, too, imagining what it must have been like. The noise of the train. His screams. The pain. "Anyway, that's what happened to his foot."

"Do you know if he knows a pair of male twins?"

"Are you joking?"

"No."

"Male twins?"

"Yes."

"No, he doesn't."

"What did he think of Curtis?"

"If I told you, I'd be incriminating him."

"I'd appreciate it if you just told me the truth."

"He thought he was a vain, shallow showboat. Robert has a real respect for the news—that's why he's kept Dev Robards on the payroll despite Dev's ratings. David was the antithesis of what Robert respects." She looked out the window. The traffic noise grew louder briefly, then faded again. "I'm getting kind of tired."

I stood up. Went over to her. Took her in my arms. But

she didn't want to kiss me. Was stiff beneath my hands.

"I'm sorry for ruining our evening," I said.

"I thought it was me."

"No, it was me. With my questions."

"I love him. I can't help it."

"I know."

"I wish I could break free. . . . I'll be forty-seven this July."

"That isn't so old."

"It isn't so young, either."

There was more traffic. She let herself drift against me; I felt her tender skin and put my face into her hair and closed my eyes. I wanted her again in a sleepy way, wanted to feel good for a moment or two as I had there in our darkness.

When I opened my eyes and looked down to the street and saw it—I thought I must be imagining it. But it shone in the street, parked as discreetly as possible between two infinitely lesser examples of the automobile. The black XKE.

"God," I said.

"What is it?"

I went to the bed. Began tugging on my clothes. "I have to go."

"Is everything all right?"

"Yes."

"Why are you moving so fast?"

"Look downstairs. There's a black XKE."

She went over and looked. "What're you going to do?" she asked.

"I'm not sure," I said. And I wasn't.

16

A LOW FOG SWAM THROUGH THE CHILLED AIR, making the shapes of houses indistinct.

I used the rear exit of Kelly's apartment house, taking the steps quickly. In back was a yard with clotheslines that I had to stoop under in the murk. The alley was gravel. The end of the block was lost in the fog. I had the impression of being in a tunnel that had no end.

I reached the beginning of Kelly's block and looked as far up the street as I could. From what I could see, he was still parked there across from her place. Watching. Waiting. I wasn't sure for what.

I was both angry and afraid. Dave Curtis's murder was baffling; about all I was sure of was that the Tomlin kid wasn't guilty. Several people whom Edelman wasn't even investigating seemed to have reasonably good motives for having killed the anchorman. And there was the man in the black XKE. Whoever he was. Whatever he wanted.

I got on his side of the street behind a tree and began to carefully make my way up the block. As I got closer I started to recognize the indistinct sounds of a car radio. His. The street was deserted enough, the fog thick enough, the blooming spring vegetation wild enough to make me feel almost lost in a bayou. My heart worked harder than it should have because I was frightened. Every former cop has stories of a buddy who approached the wrong car on the wrong night and got his face blown away. You get leery as you get older. I had no idea what I'd find when I got there.

The XKE was running. Its powerful but overly sensitive engine thrummed in the gloom. I was close enough to see the faint green glow of the dashboard through the rear window. I picked up a large rock that would give my punch the effect of a blackjack.

I got down off the curb doing my duck squat and paused. I could see the shape of his head. Staring straight ahead. Smoking a cigarette. Fog rolled around his car like currents on the bottom of the ocean. The night kept the sound of his car radio indistinct. For a moment I had the sense that this was all a nightmare. It had that quality. But I was sweating and I had to go to the bathroom and I was scared in an oddly exhilarating way. It was real. I hefted the rock again and got ready to move.

The sonofabitch was a mastermind.

I was no more than two feet from his rear bumper when the XKE door flew open and a big bald guy wearing a fashionable leather topcoat pulled six feet five of himself to the pavement and put a Magnum on range with the middle of my forehead.

"You ain't exactly quiet, you stupid bastard," he said.

He came over. He seemed to be enjoying himself. Fog swirled around him like smoke. In the streetlight I couldn't quite make out his features, just that for all his flashy style they were brutal.

"I want the tapes," he said.

The dampness wasn't doing much for my voice. Neither

was his Magnum. "I don't know what you're talking about."

He crossed to me in no more than three steps, picked me up with impressive ease and slammed me against the back of his XKE.

"I want the tapes, asshole, and I want them now."

All I could think of were the videotapes that Kelly Ford had in her office, the ones of Curtis interviewing the kid. But I had the feeling that these weren't the tapes the man was after. "I don't have them.'

"Then you know who's got them?"

"I don't even know what tapes you're talking about."

"Motherfucker." He slammed me against the car again, and this time he put the cold hard end of the piece just above my nose. "She got it?"

"Who?"

He nodded across the street.

I had to take the chance. He had me pinned down with his left hand while his right held the Magnum. I took the only chance I had. With my left hand I dug my fingers deep enough into his left eye to feel it start to swim free of its socket. With my right hand I slammed the barrel of the Magnum away from my head.

It exploded so loudly that I lost all hearing as I dove for the fog and darkness behind the big elm where I'd been hiding.

The Magnum had blown out his back window. You could hear the neighborhood come alive, see the lights behind the gloom, sense the terror.

"You motherfucker," he said, and started after me.

He wasn't worth a damn as a tracker. Not any more than I had been sneaking up on him. He stepped through bushes and made enough noise to scare away all the animals in a seven-mile radius. He tripped on the sidewalk and swore.

And his leather coat reminded me of the squeaking of bedsprings in a motel for adulterers.

I kept moving backward toward the point where, somewhere in the fog, my car was waiting. I already had the keys in my hand. Ready.

We probably heard the siren at the same time. Somewhere in the night it made its way toward us, probably accompanied by some very pissed-off police officers. This was a respectable middle-class neighborhood. You didn't go around firing Magnums in it.

"Shit," he said.

I was behind a bush. Watching him.

He stamped a foot like a peeved little boy, jammed the big gun into his coat and then started running back to his car. He made an impressive spectacle running like that. Put you in mind of a deft-footed fullback.

I felt my way through the scents of grass and apple blossoms and coldness and found my car.

He hit the street about five yards ahead of me, his lights slashing the gloom, his tires peeling out stuntman style on the pavement.

I went after him. He knew something I didn't. That was one reason. And he'd pissed me off. I hadn't looked real sharp sneaking up on him, nor had I looked real sharp decorating the back of his XKE while he held a gun to my head. Most of us don't like to be reminded that we're less good at our chosen calling than we think we are.

Two blocks away the fog lifted somewhat, and then I really got on his ass. I swooped up behind him on the damp streets at eighty miles an hour. At first he didn't know what to do, so he did something very stupid. He leaned out the window and took a shot at me. The explosion claimed the left half of my windshield. For a guy who had a vested interest in the police not finding us, this guy was none too bright. On the other hand, maybe he didn't need or even want to be bright. As a cop I'd met many men who had no brains. But they had cunning and they had hatred, and sometimes those things will take you much farther than brains.

He fishtailed around a corner and I saw then, the wide way he took it, that he wasn't much of a driver. He must have had the idea that we were in a TV show, maybe "The Rockford Files" with all its car chases, and we were going to make our cars do things they'd never done before. But it wasn't that way at all. Right now we were very dangerous and stupid citizens endangering the lives of many other citizens by shooting up and down narrow streets that were meant for thirty-mph traffic at best.

His next trick was to jam on the brakes hard enough to make a ninety-degree turn and go down an alley.

There was no way I could stop, and for a time I lost him. At the head of the block I pulled into the curb and killed my lights. I sat there sweating and panting and cursing. I had to piss so bad I had the terrible uncomfortable feeling that I was going to wet my pants, and I was shaking so bad from nerves that even the soles of my feet were wet. He wasn't worth a shit as a stunt-car man and neither was I, but for some reason we were trying to prove otherwise to each other.

He came back out of the alley a few moments later. He was driving fast but not too fast. He didn't see me at all until I jerked on my headlights two blocks later. Under the foggy streetlight his blasted-out back window looked obscene. He shot at me again.

I floored my gas petal. He responded by hitting maybe a hundred miles an hour. This time he was going to get rid of me and for good.

Then we hit the intersection. I saw the semi before he did. Even if he had seen it, it wouldn't have mattered.

He went under it or tried to—or that's what it looked like, anyway—and just when he hit it the roof sheered off. Then the car kept going beneath the semi and I didn't see anything, just heard things: shattering glass and tearing metal and the big semi trying to stop.

I got my own car over to the side of the intersection and reacted without really considering what I was doing.

The intersection ran north-south to an old highway. On all four sides were businesses shut down for the night. In the fog the XKE's lights shot straight up into the air like a beacon. I got over to the semi and looked up at the driver. He just sat behind his wheel and rubbed his face as if none of this were real. He could have been crying. I couldn't tell for sure.

I'd brought my flashlight with me. I knew I had to work quickly. I got down on my knees beneath the trailer of the semi and started crawling in. There was a suffocating smell of gas and car oil. Sticking out from where the door had been I saw a hand. I swallowed and kept going. When I was fully under the trailer, I saw that gas was leaking from the tank to the ground. Now I had to worry not only about the arrival of the authorities but an explosion.

I pushed my hands inside the mangled door and pulled him out. His face looked as if somebody had worked it over with razor blades. He was meat and blood and bone and nothing more at all. Cop instinct had me reach over and feel for a pulse. You never knew. But I knew now, of course. He was dead.

I had a minute or two at best. I tried his back pocket first and that was a mistake for two reasons. First, I had to waste time jamming my hand between his body and the car seat.

Second, he didn't carry a billfold. Instead he carried a wallet, and I found it, sweaty and anxious, moments later inside his fancy leather coat. I didn't take all his ID, but I did take everything but his driver's license and money.

The gas leak was getting worse. I pulled myself out from the wreckage, drenched in gas, car oil and blood. By the time I struggled to my feet again, lost once more in the fog, I heard a siren nearby and I saw a face even closer.

The truck driver, a tall guy who looked as if he could probably tell you more than you cared to know about the history of the Grand Ole Opry, said, "There somebody else in that car?"

I just started walking away. I'd gotten what I'd come for.

He grabbed me. Spun me around. "Hey, this is serious shit, mister. I asked if there was somebody else in that car."

I ripped his hand away from me. "He's dead, and it wasn't your fault and when the police look at the accident they'll see that it wasn't your fault. Okay?" I felt sorry for him. I was being a prick. But I couldn't help it. I needed to be out of there. Fast.

"Goddammit, he's fuckin' dead!" the driver said. He was obviously a good man, and this was all bullshit he didn't deserve.

"It'll be all right. You weren't responsible in any way. All right?"

"He's fuckin' dead?"

This is not an uncommon reaction at traffic accidents. Shock and guilt. We're a lot more fragile than the macho boys let on.

I patted him on the shoulder again. I didn't know what else to do. The siren was drawing nearer.

Then I broke into a run and got into my car and got out of there.

17 BEFORE I DID ANYTHING ELSE I TOOK A shower, and then I had a long solitary drink. I stood in clean underwear by the window looking out at the fog rolling beneath the streetlight. A shabby little room for a shabby little life. The fog didn't make it any better.

I left his wallet on the table and watched a little TV—a rerun of a "Larry Kane Show"—and I let myself doze off. When I woke up four hours later, I was covered with sweat, and at first I wasn't sure where I was; then I remembered the accident, the noise of it mostly, and then I looked across the room at the table and the guy's wallet.

Light was in the window now, early morning light, and the sound of birds pressed against the glass, and in the far left corner of my only window, like a perspective detail in a painting, there was the branch of an elm tree, green and blooming and at the moment looking pretty fucking wonderful. It cheered me up idiotically, and I let myself fall back on the couch and have two more—and much less troubled—hours of sleep. The fog world was behind me.

Knocking woke me, and even through my sleep it seemed familiar knocking, something about the cadence of his knuckle rapping this door in just this way.

You would think that in an efficiency apartment this small I'd have had no trouble finding pants or a robe, but I couldn't find either. So I just wrapped a blanket around myself and went to the door. I opened it only a crack.

"God, are you all right?" Donna Harris said.

Before I could say anything, her eyes narrowed and she looked at me with something like x-ray vision. It was very still there in my ancient dusty hallway, with just the birds for background.

She looked lovely. She was beautiful in a suburban sort of way, and yet exotic, too, thanks to her one slightly straying eye. In her brown corduroy car coat and starched button-down white shirt she managed to be both schoolgirlish and erotic. But then she trembled as tears came to her eyes, and she said, "You did it, didn't you?"

"What?"

"He came over last night and asked me if I would but I wouldn't. Out of fairness to you, I told him."

"Donna, what are you talking about?" But in a terrible way I already knew what she was talking about.

"I don't blame you though." She was gibbering.

"Do you want to come inside?"

"I mean it's all my fault. It really is. Being so indecisive."

"If you come inside I'll make some Nestlé's hot chocolate."

"I don't know why I'm the way I am."

136

I put out my hand. She didn't take it.

"I knew it would have to happen. I mean I knew you could only wait around so long."

"I love you, Donna."

"And I don't have any right at all to be jealous."

One of my neighbors, a widow whose room was a museum of WWII mementos, shuffled by in fuzzy slippers and shot me a smile, and then looked at Donna and her tears and gave me a scowl as if it were all my fault.

"Come on inside, Donna, please."

"I guess I'm naive."

"It's one of the things I love about you."

"I'm thirty-six and I've only slept with fourteen men."

"That isn't very many."

"I don't have any right to cry or be jealous, Dwyer. We had an agreement. We're adults."

"Sometimes we're adults."

"But I *am* hurt."

"I know," I said.

"And I'm pissed off, too."

"I can see that."

"I'd like to slap you."

"I've got that coming."

"Don't be smug."

"I'm not trying to be smug. It's just that I don't know what to say. You took one look at me and knew what I did last night, and now I don't know what to say."

"I would only let Chad kiss me on the lips. I wouldn't even let him French kiss me. And he's my own ex-husband. This wasn't your ex-wife you were with by any chance?"

"I'm afraid not."

"Shit, Dwyer."

I put out my hand again, and this time she took it and

came inside. She sat on the very edge of the couch as if she didn't plan to stay more than two or three seconds, and then she started crying, really wailing, and I went over and opened the window and got some beautiful morning breeze and sunlight and birdsong in the place, thinking or at least hoping it would help, but it didn't. She just kept on sobbing, pausing only once to say, "Jealousy's so goddamned unbecoming," and then going right on with her tears.

"You want them over easy?"

"This doesn't make any sense."

"I need to do some damn thing, Dwyer. I really do. So I'm making you breakfast."

"I hurt you, Donna. I didn't mean to, but that was the net effect. So the last thing I expect is for you to make me breakfast."

"Then I'm going to scramble the goddamn things."

Which is what she did. Sort of anyway. About halfway through her Betty Crocker routine she got to crying again, and then she really got pissed and started slamming things around. As a consequence my eggs had sharp little pieces of shell in them and my toast was black. "I hope you're going to be gentleman enough to keep your girlfriend's identity to yourself."

"She's hardly my girlfriend."

"I just hope it's nobody I know."

"You and I don't know anybody in common."

"In this crummy world, Dwyer, you can never be sure."

She banged down the plate with the bacon on it, then dropped the jam jar from a height of two feet. She sat down and put her lovely hurt face in her skinny hands and looked at me and said, "I'm being a baby, aren't I?"

"Not really."

"You had every right to sleep with her."

"Yeah. That's what you said."

"I guess I just thought you'd give me a little more time before you slept with anybody."

"Now I wish I had. I made a mistake. I care about you too much to fuck things up this way."

"You had every right though."

"If you say that again, I'm going to step on your foot. Hard."

"It's true."

"Just shut up, okay?"

"Okay."

She sat there and watched me finish off my breakfast. When I got to the bacon, she said, "Boy, that's where we're really different. When I really let somebody down, the last thing I can do is eat."

"The way you hand out the guilt messages, you should have been a nun."

"After what you did last night, maybe I'll consider it."

I got up and went over and kissed her.

"You've got jam on your mouth," she said, and then she started crying again and then she grabbed me and pulled me to her and kissed me really hard.

We made love on the sleeper.

"I'm sorry about what I did last night."

"Let's talk about something else now. Okay?"

"Okay," I said.

We were there in the sunlight among the mussed sheets. The birds were at it again. I smelled pleasantly of breakfast and of Donna.

"Tell me about David Curtis getting murdered," she said. "That's really weird."

So I did, and it kind of helped me get everything into perspective again.

I told her about hearing Mitch Tomlin on the second floor of Channel 3. I told her about being in the lunchroom with Kelly Ford when Curtis died. I told her that the killer had put cyanide in Curtis's laxative. Then I described chasing Tomlin's friend Diane Beaufort and how that had led me to Falworthy House and Karl Eler. I told her that while Edelman had had no choice but to arrest Mitch Tomlin, I thought the real killer was to be found among the Channel 3 staff. Mike Perry, the sportscaster, had a violent temper and had been humiliated by Curtis. Dev Robards was slowly being phased out by David Curtis. Robert Fitzgerald was a man losing his station to debt; he was desperate and maybe had a reason to kill Curtis that I hadn't uncovered yet. Bill Hanratty had some sort of connection with a sinister man in a black XKE, who had been killed last night during a chase.

"You mentioned somebody but didn't make her a suspect."

"Who?" I said. If her radar was good enough to pick up that I'd been unfaithful, then maybe she knew by some weird intonation in my voice that I'd been unfaithful with Kelly Ford.

"Marcie Grant."

"Why would she kill Curtis?" I asked.

She shrugged a beautiful bare shoulder. "She was the producer of the series about suicide. And that sounds funny to me."

"What does?"

"Oh, maybe she was jealous that Curtis got all the glory or something."

"Doubtful."

She sighed. "This is really confusing, isn't it?"

"Yeah it is."

"And I'm not being much help."

"Sure you are. Just your talking about it helps me."

"You're sweet."

"There's something that bothers me about it all, and I still don't know what."

"I have the same feeling."

We didn't say anything for a long time. I got sentimental about her in the silence.

"How's the paper going?" I asked her.

"Pretty good."

"I'm sorry about last night."

"I know."

"And I love you."

"I know that, too. And I love you."

"Are you going to see Rex today?"

"Rex is an asshole."

"That makes me happy to hear."

"He really is."

"Hey, you don't have to convince me."

"I should charge him instead of him charging me. As if I don't have enough problems already."

"No argument there."

She frowned. "You didn't need to say that."

After I dropped her off, I drove downtown. The radio had stories about the truck accident and then about how Mitch Tomlin was being held on a quarter-of-a-million-dollar bond. All I could think of was the kid sitting in the cell with the type of cons you tend to meet in a county lockup. The poor bastard.

18

ACCORDING TO THE ID I'D LIFTED FROM THE dead man last night, his name had been Thomas Ross and he'd been a private detective with a firm named Allied Investigations. Allied was the first place I went.

I found it in one of those old bank buildings that house a myriad of tiny operations ranging from chiropractors to phone solicitation services. Allied was on the third floor behind a frosted glass door that was straight out of a Dick Powell mystery movie from the forties. It was locked and when I put my ear to it, the only sound I heard was that of the elevator whining downward behind me.

I tried the doorknob again to see if it would give at all. Nothing. I walked down the wide wooden hallway that smelled of dust and floor wax to another pebbled glass door that announced WORTHINGTON CLAIMS ADJUSTMENTS.

Behind a Royal manual typewriter at least forty years old sat a fat woman who appeared to be at least seventy years old. In an ashtray burned a cigarillo, and by her hand stood a long glass whose contents were suspiciously amber. She was either drinking a urine sample or tippling. I guessed the latter. She had grandma-white hair with an irritated red scalp and a lot of white facial hair. She wore a faded housedress that hid maybe two hundred and fifty pounds of weight. She typed with two fingers, and didn't see me at first, and when she did, she didn't look happy. "Help you?" she said. Obviously I'd interrupted her typing.

"Wonder if you could tell me a few things about the man down the hall?"

"Which man? The business-consultant fella or the detective-agency fella."

"The detective-agency fella."

"Why?"

"He was killed last night."

"No shit, kemo sabe."

"He was working on a case for a lady friend of mine, a very discreet case, and she'd like to get her file back."

"She would, eh?"

"Yes, she would. So I just wondered if Mr. Ross had any associates he worked with."

"None that I know of."

"I see."

"So I guess your lady friend's out of luck."

I kind of doffed an invisible hat to her. "Yes, I guess she is. Well, thank you."

"You bet."

Before I had stepped foot over her threshold, she had picked up the amber glass and tasted deeply of it. I had the sense that she'd been trapped up here since 1947. If you'd asked her, she'd have probably told you that Harry Truman was president.

I didn't have much choice. I put my years of police training to good use by waiting until I saw that the hall was perfectly empty and then breaking into Allied Investigations. I used a pick and it took five minutes.

The furniture inside surprised me. Very expensive leather stuff. A matched set with the XKE. Maybe Ross stayed in this old building because the rent was right. Spring sunlight gave the air a golden dusty laziness. I went over to the dry bar and looked at the contents. A lot of Wild Turkey. Ross had been a high roller.

The filing cabinets were inside a walk-in closet. There were three of them and they promised to hold the secrets of the ages. The dirty secrets. It took me ten minutes to find the first name that held any interest. The name was Robert Fitzgerald, the owner of Channel 3.

During the next five minutes I found several manila folders marked with names, including David Curtis, Kelly Ford, Marcie Grant, Bill Hanratty, Dev Robards, Mike Perry and the dead boy, Stephen Chandler. I gathered them up and was coming out of the closet when I heard the step on the wood floor outside.

She said, "Come out and be careful."

When I got out there she was holding a large and very old .45 on me. In the lazy sunlight she looked fifty pounds fatter and aged in a sick sort of way.

"This belonged to the mister," she said. Which seemed to amuse her in some way. "He said I'd be able to use it someday."

I really like inexperienced people pointing guns at me. "You don't need it," I said.

"Maybe you're dangerous."

"I told you. I needed a file for a friend."

She nodded to my arms, where several files were stacked haphazardly. "Looks like you've got more friends than one."

"Really," I said, "you don't need the gun."

"Maybe what I need is money."

"What's that mean?"

"It means I could always call the cops and get you arrested on a B and E."

I sighed. In movies PIs walk around with enough cash in their pockets to pay off half the U.S. Congress. At any given time in my pockets I had ten dollars. At least this morning I had my checkbook.

"If you put the gun down, I'll write you a check for five dollars."

She laughed hoarsely. "Jesus Christ, bud, you're really the last of the big-time spenders."

"Ma'am, I'm not wealthy."

"I want more than five."

"How about seven?"

"Seven goddamn dollars?"

I knew she was going to get me up to ten. I just thought I'd haggle and try to contain the damage.

"A girl like me needs money," she said. She was being coy. With her white facial hair and her whiskey-red face, coy didn't quite work.

"Eight-fifty," I said.

"Ten."

"Ten bucks?"

"Ten goddamn bucks or I keep the gun up and I call the cops."

Two minutes later I sat behind Ross's desk writing out a check. "How do you spell your last name?" I asked.

"Pournelle. P-o-u-r-n-e-l-l-e."

I tore off the check, blew on it to dry the ink and handed it over. She looked at it as if she was studying a dollar bill for evidence of counterfeit.

"Just who the hell are you?"

"Does it matter?" I said. "You've got your money."

"Ten crummy bucks, bud."

"Ten bucks is what I budget myself for lunch and dinner. It means I eat whatever the change in my pocket will buy me."

"Go to McDonald's."

"You don't go to McDonald's with change these days. You need several dollar bills."

"So why would you break into Ross's? Really."

"I told you. For a friend."

From a large pocket in her housedress she took a half-pint bottle of cough syrup and tipped it up to her mouth.

"For my ten dollars do I get to ask you any questions?"

"Depends on what they are."

"What kind of work did Ross do?"

"Like it says on the door, he was a private investigator."

"Yeah, but I mean what kind? Did he do mostly security work, divorce work, corporate work—what?"

She smiled unpleasantly. "Him and the twins liked to have fun when they worked."

Her mention of the twins made me dizzy with all the possibilities. "The twins?"

She nodded. "John and Rick. You ever see them?"

"No."

"They could be movie stars. Identical twins and just as handsome as Tyrone Power used to be."

"They worked with Ross?"

"All the time. And like I said, they liked to have fun on their jobs."

"What does that mean?"

The smirk stayed. "Let's just say they took a lot of pleasure in their work. You can ask a downtown businessman about that."

Her dramatic pauses irritated me. "I'm not going to write you another check."

"You're a cheap bastard."

"There are worse things to be."

"They cut up his buttocks."

"Whose buttocks?"

"The businessman."

"They cut up his buttocks?"

"Yeah. There's this fat lawyer whose wife fucks half the people in the bars downtown. He's used to it by now. But with this one businessman she got serious. So the lawyer got mad and hired the twins. They took a butcher knife and cut the guy's buttocks in long strips. He wasn't able to sit down for months. He never bothered the lawyer's wife again. Of course, by now she's back to fucking everybody who walks through the door."

"They sound like fun guys."

"The twins?"

"Yeah."

"They're very pretty and you might think they're queers, but if you ever saw them in action you'd think otherwise, believe me." The note of admiration in her voice was as chilling as the lawyer anecdote she'd just related.

I sat there in the sunlight and wished to hell I did something else for a living. You hang around too many people like this old babe here and you begin to think everybody's like her.

I picked up the files and walked around the desk. She started to reach for the .45 in her pocket again, but I just frowned and said, "I'm going is all."

"You taking those with you?" She meant the files.

"Yeah."

"I should charge you more."

I gave her my best glare. "You've pushed your luck about as far as it's going to go."

She looked me over and decided I was serious and then just gave me a great cynical shrug and let me walk past her and out into the gloom of the hallway.

19

DOWNSTAIRS IN THE LOBBY I TRIED BECKER, but Bobby Lee said he was tied up. "Am I going to get some work for tonight?"

Our brief friendship from yesterday was gone. She was back to her old self. "You really embarrassed the agency, that kid getting into Channel Three while you were on duty."

"So I'm not going to be working tonight?"

"Not till further notice."

I hung up.

At home I spread the files out and went through them one by one. Two hours later I still had no real idea what I was looking at.

In Robert Fitzgerald's file, for example, there was a neatly typed note that said, *Obviously he was the main force behind the whole thing.*

What whole thing?

In both Hanratty and Robards' file the same language appeared. *Paid them each $1000. Both provided me with information.*

What kind of information?

Something was going on here, something that seemed to link the Channel 3 people in some way more binding than merely working together—but what?

I made some instant coffee and sat in the sunlight and thought again about getting a cat (my boy still had the family cat) and tried to guess what Ross's notes were about, but I couldn't.

I decided to drive over to Falworthy House before going out to see Kelly Ford.

Karl Eler looked sweatier and more desperate than ever when I arrived. He had a stolid and hostile-looking boy in his office and was trying to make a point to him. "The man from the juvenile bureau is very mad, Ronnie. Very mad. You stayed out past your curfew last night and they picked you up. They could send you to reform school."

"Fuck 'em."

You could sense poor Eler writhing inside. Trying to help people who didn't care if they were helped or not. Being Jesus is never easy. It wasn't even easy for Jesus himself.

"Ronnie," he said, and wrung his hands, literally. Ronnie frowned, obviously seeing Eler as less than a man. "Go back to your room," Eler said. He spoke in a whisper.

Ronnie got up, kind of scratched his balls, kind of shook his head at the pathetic sight of Eler and went out of the room.

When Eler saw me, he said, "I've started looking around."

"Looking around?"

"For other jobs."

"It getting to you?"

He ran a miserable hand over his miserable face. "Everything's getting to me, I'm afraid. I'm forty years old. I've lost my wife, I don't have much hair left and for the first time I'm starting to worry about things like cancer and heart disease. I don't need this kind of torture on top of it."

"Some of the kids here are pretty nice, for whatever that's worth."

He looked melancholy a moment. "Yes, some of them are nice, and some of them appreciate what I try to do for them. But a lot of them . . ." He shook his head again. "Well, what can I do for you today?"

I had become one of his students. He treated me with professional interest and a certain haste.

"I'd like to see Diane again if I could."

"Of course. This is one of her work-internship days at Hardee's, and she's still upstairs getting ready. I'll get her."

I looked at my nickle notepad, on which I'd written down several points. After he called upstairs for Diane, I said, "Did you ever see any older men hanging around here waiting for Stephen Chandler?"

"No. I would have objected if I had. What with all the perversion in the world, I'm not about to stand for things like that."

"Did Stephen ever mention anything to you about any of the people he might have been hanging out with away from Falworthy House?"

He thought a moment. "Not that I recall."

"He never mentioned twins?"

"No."

I closed my notebook and turned to see Diane. She looked tired. Her prettiness was washed out. I wanted to give her a little hug and buy her some breakfast. At the moment she needed a parent. And I needed a child.

"You can go into the sunroom," Eler suggested. Obviously he had other work he wanted to get back to.

We went into the sunroom.

She sat on the edge of a couch that was ratty with age. The light was dusty and melancholy.

"I kept having dreams about him," she said. I assumed she was talking about Mitch Tomlin in jail. "God, I really loved him. I wish he hadn't killed himself."

All I could do was watch, wait.

She allowed herself a few terrible tears, as if there were an alloted number she couldn't exceed, and then she started biting on the edge of one already badly bitten nail, and then she started snuffling.

"I need to ask you a few more questions."

"I think I helped kill him," she said.

"No, you didn't, Diane."

"Toward the last, when he was flying so high, I should have seen that he was just covering up how depressed he was."

"That's what I wanted to talk to you about."

"What?"

"When Stephen was flying high."

"Okay." She looked curious, even a bit afraid of my business-like tone.

"You remember the twins you mentioned?"

"Yes."

"I'm trying to find them."

"Why?"

"Because they can help me prove that Mitch didn't kill Curtis."

"Really?"

I nodded.

"Well," she said, "I did see something kind of weird one night." She bit at a fingernail, then went on. "I went up to his room upstairs to talk to him, see if we couldn't get back together and all, but he was getting dressed up. You know how I told you about all the new clothes he'd gotten and everything and nobody could figure out where he was getting the money?"

I nodded.

"Well, anyway, he's getting dressed up in this really fancy silk shirt and some new leather pants and when I got inside his room he looked real uncomfortable, like it was really a drag to see me. Anyway, I started to talk, but he said he was in a hurry and couldn't talk, that some people were waiting down on the corner for him. I thought that was real weird, you know, that they'd wait down on the corner instead of out front. So he just brushed past me. I tried to grab him and get him to hold me, but he just looked at me like I was this pain-in-the-ass-little kid, you know, and then he half ran out of the house. I followed him. It was dark out—it was probably eight o'clock or something—and I followed him down the block and then I saw this really incredible car, this red car, it was older but it was really shiny, I think it was a Cadillac, and in the streetlight I could make out these two guys sitting in the front seat, and it was very strange but I got the impression they were both the same guy. I mean the way they sat and the way they wore their hair and the clothes they wore, everything. It was like looking at a —what's that word—it's like clown or something?"

"Clone."

"Yeah, like looking at a clone."

"But he never said anything about them directly?"

"No."

"Did he ever mention anything to you about a tape?"

"What kind of tape?"

"I'm not sure. Maybe an audiotape."

An unlikely and beautiful grin parted her lips suddenly. "Audiotape. Oh, yeah. He was always talking about his tapes. That's right."

"What kind of tapes?"

"He said he wanted to be a writer someday but he didn't know how to type very good, so he'd just put everything down on tape. He always got real high marks in English composition and stuff, especially when he wrote about his life. The teachers were always telling him he should keep on writing about himself because he was so good at it."

I was beginning to see why Ross had been interested in the tapes—not the videotapes of Curtis's interview with Stephen Chandler, but audiotapes that Chandler had kept as a diary. "Do you know where he kept his tapes?"

"In his room, I suppose."

"I imagine by now they've moved his stuff."

"Yeah. It's probably in the basement."

"Why would it be there?"

"That's where Karl moved Stephen's clothes and stuff. He was going to give them all away but I talked him out of it. It's kind of nice for some reason, having them around I mean."

God, I liked her. "How about taking me to the basement?"

"Sure. You think Karl will mind?"

"Probably. But let's go anyway."

The grin again.

The basement was divided into sections with pine board and chicken wire. It smelled of dust and dampness, but not unpleasantly so. When you grew up in basements like this, you find yourself missing them in this era of ranch-style houses.

Stephen Chandler's clothes took up one small corner. Just touching the clothes—the suede jackets and pants, the silky shirts—I saw why it was so odd that Stephen should have had things like this. There was no way he could have afforded them. Legally anyway. I wondered if he hadn't been helping the twins do something that got to be too much for him, like dealing drugs maybe, and then killed himself when guilt and fear overtook him. Stephen had clearly never been very stable.

She found a box of tapes in the back, a neat stack of cassettes in a shoe box. She handed them over sadly and with reverence. "God, don't lose these, okay?"

"Don't worry." I leaned over and kissed her on the forehead. "When this is all over, I'm going to take you and Mitch out to a great dinner."

"You really thing Mitch is going to get out?"

"You bet he is."

Fifteen minutes later, a familiar voice on the other end of the phone was saying, "Good morning, *Ad World*."

"Good morning yourself. I've been thinking about you," I said.

"I've been thinking about you, too. I'm going to do us both a favor and really resolve this thing one way or another with my ex-husband and to hell with Rex."

"To hell with Rex?" I said.

"Yeah. I think all his theorizing—not to mention his subtle little sexual advances—is just messing me up all the more."

"I'm glad to hear you say that."

"Were you ever jealous of Rex?"

"All the time."

"Are you serious?"

"Yeah."

"Jeeze, you really are a jealous person, aren't you?"

"It's because I'm so insecure."

"What are you insecure about?"

"You want to start with the As and work through the alphabet?"

She laughed. "Dwyer, you are really a fine man, you really are."

"Thank you. Now I want to ask you for some help." I told her about the tapes I'd just found, and I told her about where they might lead us.

"God," she said.

"So could you spend the rest of the day listening to them? I've got too many appointments."

"Sure. I didn't have much to do anyway."

"Good. I'll drop them by."

"Thanks for asking me." She sounded as if she'd just won an Academy Award.

"Thanks yourself," I said.

20

MEDIA ASSOCIATES WAS HOUSED IN A THREE-story red-brick building that had been refurbished into a rather trendy showplace. Volvos, BMWs and Audis disguised as Mercedeses filled the lot that took up three sides. Among Ross's files on the Channel 3 people I'd found some very interesting documents. I brought them with me in a briefcase.

A sneering guard in a military-type security uniform checked me in with a trace of pity in his eyes for the ten-year-old Harris Tweed jacked I wore. The military ambience continued with a stern-looking receptionist, who forced me to sign in and wear a little plastic badge with VISITOR stamped on it. She escorted me down a long hall to Kelly Ford's office.

On the way we passed maybe a dozen young men in look-alike three-piece suits. They exuded that arrogance that comes to people who spend their lives at superficial tasks for far too much reward. They protected their secrets by wearing corporate camouflage—didn't any of these fuckers get their shoes scuffed?—and saving their passion not for bed or art but for advancement. They were toadies, and the worst thing of all was that they didn't realize they were toadies.

When I appeared in her doorway, Kelly Ford was working at a big IBM electric typewriter with the skill of a champion secretary. When she heard me say "Hi" and turned my way, there was a sad little smile pulling at her mouth. She was embarrassed. "Well, hi," she said far too effusively. She even got up and shot out her hand for me to shake. "Why don't you sit down and let me finish this letter? Would you mind?"

What could I say? As I sat there looking around her small but very well-appointed office—just once I'd like to see one of the big corporations hang silk paintings of dogs and Elvis and stuff like that—I realized she'd hurt my feelings. What we'd done last night had been a little understandable grudge fucking. I was feeling sorry for myself about Donna Harris, she was feeling sorry for herself about Robert Fitzgerald. Our respective griefs should have bound us together in at least a tenuous way. But all she had for me this morning was remorse disguised as officiousness.

She was rolling along and I couldn't resist. "How you doing?"

She stopped typing and looked up. "Me?"

"Sure. You."

"I'm doing just fine. How are you doing?"

"I'm doing fine, too."

She looked perplexed and irritated. "Well, that's nice." Then she went back to her typing.

It was a lovely way to spend ten minutes, and by the time she paid attention to me again, I felt as badly about last night as she did. We'd grudge fucked, all right, except by the dawn's early light the guy she had a grudge against was me.

She turned around and took a big corporate smile from

the drawer and fitted it expertly over her mouth. "Sorry," she said, nodding to the typewriter. "Just had a little work I needed to finish up."

"Right."

"You want to see the Chandler interview videotapes, don't you?"

"Yes."

"I've got them on three-quarter-inch, so we can go into one of the conference rooms and see them there."

"Great."

"Is something wrong?"

"Not really, I guess."

"Good," she said.

And that was that.

On the way into the conference room, we passed many large windows where television newspeople were being trained.

Mind you, they weren't doing things like reading books about history or politics; they weren't out in a ghetto finding out about the impact of Reaganomics on the impoverished; no, they were sitting in rooms with TV cameras and big monitors so they could study themselves and how they looked on the tube. An actor friend of mine sick of starving to death as a thespian had gone to a place like Media Associates, and two weeks later had his first job as an anchorman. He didn't know diddly about news or news gathering, but that didn't matter—he had a face you could put on Rushmore and a lot of gray at the temples. Distinguished, you know. He liked to laugh that with his first paycheck he bought a subscription to *Time* magazine so he could find out what was going in the world. "Shit, I even have to read newspapers now, and I don't mean just the comics."

At one of the windows I stopped, because I saw Kelly Ford's image on a TV screen. On the other side of the window sat several people with notebooks taking notes. Out of the muffled sounds I heard that she had taped an instructional segment on how different kinds of attire altered the image you projected.

"Hey, wait a minute," I said. "This should be good."

She flushed. "That's one of my duties. Teaching our newsies about makeup and wardrobe."

She photographed very well; she wore a high, frilly collar and a fitted gray skirt similar to the outfit she was wearing today. Next to her on the screen stood a rather nondescript young man in a plain white shirt. First she put a blue blazer on him. He looked preppy. Then she put a tailored gray suit jacket on him and combed his disco hair into a part. He looked like an earnest young banker. Then she put a blond wig on him as well as the blazer. Except now she took off his tie and opened his shirt collar. He resembled a lounge singer. It was a fascinating process.

"I wish I had longer to spend," she said, "but I don't." She was getting bit tart. Our time together last night was drifting farther and farther away.

Before we reached the conference room, we passed several more windows that looked in on various groups having various meetings.

The last one was especially interesting to me: inside sat the entire Channel 3 news staff, including station owner Robert Fitzgerald. Another corporation clone was giving them some kind of chalk talk on a portable blackboard. "He's breaking down the new ratings," she explained. "In the last Nielson we did very well. We did even better this time. That's what he's explaining to them."

"Did your ratings improve because of the story on teenage suicide?"

"Yes," she said, "I'm happy to say they did."

He had one of those young, handsome faces that are almost too sensitive. You wanted to see him smile instead of looking so self-involved. In all I watched six different interviews with Stephen Chandler, and each one grew progressively tougher to view.

His face was in shadows, but you still got a very good idea of his looks. He spoke in a surprisingly deep voice that only cracked when he was near tears. He described a life that nobody should have had. Deserted young by father and mother. Transferred to various foster homes, in two of which he was abused. Drugs by the time he was fourteen. And then two serious suicide attempts.

The only bad part of the interview was David Curtis. He was a gag. He reminded me of my actor friend who'd become an anchorman. He sat there with his clipboard and made judgments on the kid. "Aren't you feeling just a little sorry for yourself? Isn't that why you take drugs?" And "Isn't it true that you broke into some houses to support your drug habit?" And finally, "Didn't you once attack one of your foster fathers with a butcher knife?" Even if the accusations were true, they obviously weren't what the kid needed to hear. At one point, sobbing, Stephen Chandler said, "I've screwed it up, I've screwed everything up." You could hear the high, hard edge of despair in his voice. Just looking at the kid made you think of melodramatic left-behind notes and wrists that were opened like silent mouths by razor blades.

But the real star was David Curtis, of course, and that's the way it was structured. He kept referring pompously to "The Channel Three investigation," as if Channel 3 were akin to the Vatican, and he kept giving us a lot of sob-sister horseshit that he delivered right into the camera. He was so hammy he made Geraldo Rivera look sincere by comparison.

"Bastard," I said in the darkness.

"What?"

"Curtis. He really pushed the kid too far. And he was a horseshit reporter to boot."

She was instantly defensive. "This series won several awards."

"Yeah, the press congratulating itself as usual on sensationalism." I was angry, and I didn't give a damn if she knew it.

She got up and shut off the TV set. She had tears in her eyes. "I thought we were friends."

"We are."

"Then you've got a strange way of showing it."

But I was just as crackling with bitterness as she was. "Yeah, like you showed back there in your office?"

"What's that supposed to mean?"

"Less than twelve hours ago we were in bed fornicating."

"Is that supposed to mean something?"

"Well, I hoped it meant a little something, anyway. Harbor in the goddamn storm if nothing else."

"I'm sorry. I was foolish. It shouldn't have happened. But that doesn't mean we can't be friends."

I stood up. I felt a bad case of the sanctimonies coming on. I wanted to grab my foot and stick it in my mouth, but it was too late. "You should drop him, Kelly. And drop this whole sleazy fucking business. All you're doing is pandering to the lowest common denominator. This isn't journalism, it's just bad show biz."

By the time I calmed down, she was already looking

away from me and toward the door. Where Robert Fitzgerald stood.

"Exactly what is he doing here, Kelly?"

"He asked to see the Chandler tapes."

"Do you know what he is, Kelly?"

She flushed. He had her cowed again as he always had
her cowed.

"He's a minimum-wage security guard who thinks he
knows more than the police do about David's death."

He took a few crippled steps into the room. He was
controlling his rage, and obviously at great cost to his
cardiovascular system.

"Now I want him out of here in two minutes and I never
want to see you with him again. Do you understand me?"

Before she could speak, I said, "Very impressive,
Fitzgerald. But you're a little late."

The others gathered near the door, listening to us—Dev
Robards, Marcie Grant, Mike Perry, Bill Hanratty.

"Kelly, I said two minutes."

"Later this afternoon I'm going to turn some files over to
the police, Fitzgerald. They belonged to a private detective
named Ross."

His flush told me all I needed to know.

He started toward me. He should have looked impressive
in his double-breasted worsted suit, but now he had reverted
to street boy, lame street boy, and you saw that he wore his
hair too long for the boardroom and there was too much
anger in the dark eyes for civilized circumstances. I should
have identified with him, felt sorry for him, I suppose. But I
didn't in the least.

From the cheap briefcase I carried I took a large manila
envelope and put it on the conference table.

"You told me your office was broken into," I said to
Kelly. "I believe these are the documents that were taken."

"What the hell is this?" Fitzgerald said. He reached for the envelope. I snatched it away. Gave it to Kelly.

"Ross knew what was going on," I said to Fitzgerald. "And very soon I will, too."

He stepped back to the phone and ripped it from its cradle. "This is Robert Fitzgerald. I want a security guard here immediately. We're in room—"

He was so furious he started to sputter. Bill Hanratty, ever the brown-nosed weatherman, said, "Room One-Fourteen D."

They stood there staring at me, the whole newsteam, and then Kelly Ford started crying and said, "Dwyer, please, please leave before it gets any worse."

It was the first time this morning that I had liked her. I reached out and touched her hip, and then I pushed my way past the others and out into the hallway.

The security guard came down with great and serious intent. I didn't want to make things difficult for him. I put my hands up in a gesture of mock surrender and said, "I'm the asshole they want to get rid of."

He had no sense of humor. "Yeah, you look like an asshole."

I was two steps from my car, enjoying the sunlight again, when I heard a familiar voice say, "I can help you with that man Ross."

I turned to find the distinguished Dev Robards coming up to me. Behind us, at the doorway, I saw Bill Hanratty watching us with great interest.

Dev's face was flushed. "Hanratty and I want to talk to you."

"You and Hanratty? I thought you didn't like him."

"I don't. But we became partners of a sort."

I nodded back to Media Associates. "What the fuck is going on here?"

"We'd like to set up an appointment with you."

"When?"

"Right after the show tonight. There's a steak house. The Castle."

"I know where it is, but it's a little expensive for what I make."

"Jesus," he said. "This is important. I'll pick up the tab."

"You're in too deep, aren't you, Dev?"

"Way too deep."

"You going to be all right?"

He shook his head. "I haven't been all right for so long, I don't think it matters."

"You wouldn't happen to know a pair of twins named Ayres, would you?"

He nodded. "Bad, bad people."

"Yeah, I kind of guessed as much."

He looked back at Media Associates. "Fitzgerald just told me that he's letting me go. They're bringing in another anchorman."

"You're a real journalist, Dev. You don't want to traffic with those jack-offs anyway."

"Jesus Christ," he said, "after all these fucking years." He cried just enough to need to blow his nose which he did with ferocity. "Now I'm almost glad we did it."

"Did what?"

"That's what we're going to tell you," he said, "tonight at The Castle."

21 IN ANOTHER HOUR I'D BE PUTTING IN HALF AN afternoon at the Guns and Ammo show. I found a Denny's, had a luncheon diet special, got a handful of change and started making phone calls, first to my agent to see if Hollywood or something resembling Hollywood had called (he mentioned the possibility of a good dinner-theater role coming up, but then he was a man who always spoke in terms of possibilities), and then to Federated to see if Becker was in (Bobby Lee coldly said no), and finally I called *Ad World* and spoke with Donna Harris.

"How's it going with the tapes?"

"God, if he didn't invent the stuff on these tapes, the Chandler kid led quite a life."

"How so?"

"A lot of girls, for one thing. At least on the tapes I've listened to so far."

"How about drugs?"

"That's the odd thing. Apparently, drugs didn't play a part in his life."

"They must've played some part. He died by overdosing on heroin."

"He talks a lot about drinking—his hero seemed to be Jack London—but almost never about taking drugs."

"Anything else?"

"The more recent tapes get sort of enigmatic. I mean on the earlier tapes he always used names and specific places, but these get very vague. He keeps talking about 'If I do what they want me to, I'll have it made, I can split for California with money in my pocket.' That's a direct quote, about splitting for California."

"Any sense of who 'they' are or what 'they' wanted him to do?"

"Not so far."

"Has he mentioned anything about the Ayres twins?"

"No." She paused. "But there's something weird about the tapes."

"What?"

"I'm not sure."

"Gee, that's helpful."

"Very funny. I just mean that I'm starting to come to some kind of conclusion, but I don't know what it's going to be yet."

"Maybe it's going to arrive on the next Federal Express shipment."

"Or maybe the woman you spent last night with is going to tell me what it is."

That kind of ended my fiesty mood.

"I'm sorry," she said.

"That's okay. We all need to take shots every once in a while."

"You were perfectly free to do whatever you wanted."

"Yeah, that's what you said."

"I called Rex and canceled my appointment."

"What did he say?"

"He must have sensed that I was really saying good-bye, because he said, 'We're just beginning to make progress, Donna. We really are.' I pay him fifty-five dollars an hour for him to hustle me, and he says we're making progress." There was another pause. "And something else happened, too."

"What?"

"Chad stopped by."

Now I knew what she must have felt like this morning when she guessed about Kelly Ford and me. "Oh?" I said. I didn't have much of a voice.

"He, uh, brought an engagement ring with him."

I didn't say anything. I couldn't.

"I had to tell you, Dwyer."

"Yeah."

"I mean I don't know what I'm going to do, how I'm going to respond. I mean, I just know that I'm being very unfair to you. I mean, I get jealous when you sleep with another woman and I have absolutely no right to."

"That's just kind of the way human beings are, I guess."

"Oh, Dwyer, God, I really care about you so much."

"Just keep listening to the tapes, okay?"

"Don't you want to say something?"

"I don't know what to say."

"Dwyer?"

"Yeah."

"You know I care about you."

"Yeah." I hung up.

I stood in the entrance to Denny's and people came by and I tried to put on little bright social smiles, but I was a mess inside. I cared about Donna in some high, clean, fine way that I hadn't cared about anybody in a long time, and I had the sense that it was soon about to end, that I was going to have my high, clean, fine feelings and absolutely nobody to use them on.

After a couple minutes of standing by the phone I took another quarter from my pocket and dropped it in the box and called my answering service. The woman who answered was excited. "You're to call a Karl Eler. He says it's an emergency."

I talked to Eler less than a half a minute later.

"My God, Dwyer, somebody came in and grabbed Diane and asked her about some tapes and then knocked her out. She's got a big goose egg and a very bad headache."

"I'll be there in ten minutes," I said.

And I was.

Eler was waiting for me in the vestibule. He looked terrible. He just kept saying "My God" as he led me up the stairs to the girls' section of Falworth. Several girls stood outside Diane's room. They might have been keeping a vigil—except for the tinny rock song on the radio.

Diane lay fully clothed on top of the covers, a damp washcloth on her head. She had rosary beads entwined in her fingers. When she saw me, she tried to smile but it just came out as a wince. Even from there I could see the purple lump just below her temple. Whoever had hit her had done it with some relish.

I stood above her, reached down and touched her shoulder. "Can you talk okay?"

"I can try," she said. She was hoarse.

"Did you get a look at them?"

She turned her head almost imperceptibly from side to side. "They had ski masks. But I know who they were."

"Who?"

"You remember what I said about that Cadillac waiting for Stephen?"

I nodded.

"How the two guys in the front seat seemed to be the same guy. Clones."

"Right."

"That's who it was. Those guys."

"The twins."

"Yes."

"What did they want?"

"Stephen's tapes."

"What did you tell them?"

She closed her very blue eyes a moment, as if gathering her courage. When she opened them, she said, "I probably got you in trouble."

"You told them I had the tapes?"

"Yes."

I reached down again and took her hand. "That's fine, honey. You did what you had to."

"I was just scared."

"We all get scared, hon. We all do what we have to."

"They'll probably come after you now."

"It's all right." I touched the washcloth. "Are you starting to feel any better?"

"A little, I guess." The eyes closed momentarily again. "I could take a little nap."

"That's a good idea."

"I really like you, Dwyer."

It was said with such innocent force that it over whelmed me momentarily.

"I really like you, too, hon."

"I like it when you call me 'hon.' I sort of remember my dad before he died. He called me 'hon.' At least I think he did. At least that's how I like to remember it."

I took her hand again. "Sleep tight." I smiled. "Hon."

Downstairs Eler paced in the vestibule. "What the hell is going on here?" he said. He looked more than ever like somebody about to literally fly apart, like a science-fiction-movie robot coming undone.

"I don't know," I said.

And the hell of it was, I didn't.

The theme of the Guns and Ammo show today was "Salute to Mercenaries." I guess if there's one type of guy I really admire, it's the big crazy galoot who takes pleasure in killing people for dollars.

Backstage I got into my survivalist getup and then went out on the floor and looked at all the fat failed dreamers walking around in their berets and gun belts and flak jackets. You never knew when you'd be walking down the street and somebody would whip out a Beretta AR70 and let you have it. During my years on the force I'd built up a real hatred for many of these people, as had most of my fellow officers. The police officer's job is dangerous enough without all these maniacs caching up enough weaponry in their basements to start WWIII.

"You look kind of down today," Lynott said.

"I guess I am."

"Anything I can help you with?"

"Nah, I guess not."

Here was this guy I should have hated—the kind of guy who took slime like Jesse Helms and Jerry Falwell seriously—the kind of guy who dreamed of blowing up cities the way other guys dreamed of humping movie stars—and I couldn't help but sort of like him. Right now, given my mood, I needed badly to hate somebody, but hard as I tried, it wasn't going to be him.

"Nah," I said, "I'll be all right."

"Must be about a woman."

"Why's that?"

"Man looks a special way when he's down about a woman."

"Well, it's partly about a woman and partly about a case I'm working on."

I had said the right word. Case. It excited him. "You working on a case?"

"Yeah."

He patted his gunbelt. "You need any firepower?"

"Maybe a couple of jet fighters in case I need to strafe a few people, but other than that I'll be all right." I could see I'd hurt his feelings. "Shit, look, I'm sorry, okay? I'm just in an asshole mood."

"Well, God knows I get in those moods, too."

"Maybe I'll go have a smoke. You mind if I take a break?"

"Not at all."

I had this notion of calling Donna Harris. For one thing I wanted to know what she'd learned about the tapes. For another I felt this need just to hear her voice.

"Well, see you in a couple minutes then," I said, and took off.

This place had been built just before WWII as part of

FDR's vast plans for employment and urban improvement. To the people of that era it must have been spectacular. Stained-glass windows detailed America's fighting men from the Revolutionary days onward. Beautiful work. I went up the stairs that tracked these windows to a small ledge where you could stand three stories up and look down into the river. I'm not fond of heights, particularly when I'm outside, but I needed some kind of charge at the moment to blast me from my funk. I stood on the ledge and looked over the city. On the backs of some of the buildings you could see faded signs that had been painted several decades earlier advertising Pepsi for a nickel and Hirschman's Tailor Shop and the Regal Hotel, and for a long moment that made me feel better. Understanding my place in the blood chain of history was just the kind of abstraction I needed to forget my more emotional problems, and probably if I hadn't been so rapt, if I hadn't been perched there right on the tip of the ledge, probably I wouldn't have been quite so frightened when it happened.

A hand shot out from behind me. Got me by the throat and held me there. "You could fucking die, pal, right fucking here, you understand?" He smelled of expensive after-shave and the sharp sweat of excitement. He was having fun with me.

I looked straight down into the muddy river and calculated my chances of surviving a fall. Eighty to twenty against, the way I saw it. Then he surprised me by jerking me back from the ledge and slamming me against the balcony wall.

At first I thought that I'd injured my head and was suffering double vision. There were two of them, and they looked so much alike they were impossible to tell apart.

They were dark-haired with the too slick handsomeness of matinee idols of the forties. They wore California sports clothes, yellow golf shirts tucked discreetly into white linen trousers. But what they most had in common wasn't what they wore; rather it was the expression in their amused dark eyes. A cynicism and urbane evil I'd never seen before. These two looked as if they were capable of performing any crime the human mind could conceive of.

One of them had a knife at my throat before I had time to slow my breathing down. "We want the tapes, asshole," he said.

"I don't have them."

"We've been looking a long time, ever since the Chandler kid died, and we're getting real tired. Now who's got them?"

"I don't know." The knife smelled of oil and clean steel. Its point penetrated flesh to the right of my Adam's apple.

He smiled. "For a security guard, man, you sure do get around."

"I used to be a cop." I knew instantly it was the wrong thing to say. Just the kind of line hip guys like these two fed on.

"Gee, a cop. I'm impressed. Aren't you impressed?" he asked his twin.

"Yeah, I'm real impressed."

"Protect and serve and all that happy horseshit."

He was spoiling the breeze. Here I was pinned at knife point to a wall, and what crossed my mind just now was how good the breeze felt.

He let me have a bit more of the knife. "You're really fucking sweating, pal," he said, the same glib amused tone in his voice.

All I could do was bug my eyes out a bit.

"I'll bet he can sweat more than that," the twin said.

"Gosh, I don't know. I've given it my best shot. You care to take a stab at it?" He grinned. "Get it? Take a 'stab' at it?"

"Guess I may as well," the twin said.

From his pocket he quick-drew a long knife identical to the one his brother held. He snicked it open and walked over. He put it up alongside his brother's knife. This close up you could see that they were vitually identical. Eerily so.

The first twin took his knife away and was starting to back off when I heard the footsteps behind them. By the time they turned, I had already had a look at who appeared.

Somehow Lynott had figured out I was in trouble and enlisted three of his fellow survivalists. The four of them in their fatigues ringed the doorway. They had enough weaponry to blow away half the city.

"Jesus Christ," the first twin said.

His brother, keeping the knife right at my throat, turned around and saw the good ol' boys. "God damn," he said.

"You two look like some kind of fruits to me," Lynott said, stepping out onto the balcony.

"Are you for real?"

"You give me half a chance, you pervert, and I'll show just how real I am."

It happened in an instant, and I only noticed it because they were standing so close to me. A kind of telepathy. One twin looked at the other, adn before anybody could do anything, they dove straight from the ledge three stories down into the water.

The four guys in the khaki uniforms took this as a perfect excuse to start a war. They stood on the ledge and fired into the water below, where the twins could be seen swimming in the rapid current. You had your ROK assault rifle. You had your Max 11 semiautomatic. You had your FAMAS submachine gun. You even had your MPRG riot gun. So many rounds were fired in so short a time that the balcony was engulfed in smoke, and I had to crush my hands to my ears to protect my hearing.

The twins, meanwhile, had gone underwater and were out of sight.

I finally got the cavalry to stop firing only by going up to Lynott and grabbing his elbow. "They're gone!" I screamed over the barrage of firepower.

"That's what they want us to think!" he screamed back.

By now, of course, there were only slightly more sirens going off in the streets below than had gone off in Berlin in the spring of 1945. The police take a decided interest when citizens decide to unleash this kind of exchange.

Lynott frowned, looking as if he'd just found out that his wife slept around. Glumly he gave the signal to the others to stop firing. They did so with the same gloomy expression. Damn but they looked disappointed.

"Now, the cops are going to be up here and asking questions. But we've got a perfectly good excuse," Lynott said. "I happened to come up here looking to see if my old buddy Dwyer was doing okay, him being pretty dejected lately and all, and I happened to see these two pretty boys holding knives on him. So I went and got some of my buddies, and by God if we didn't end up savin' Dwyer's life."

For all his hokum, he had in fact saved my life.

"I appreciate it, you guys, I really do. I mean I don't

think it was necessary to use quite as much firepower as you did, but what the fuck."

"Absolutely right. What the fuck. Just as long as you're willing to say that to the cops."

Which I did five minutes later when a couple of guys from the SWAT team plus maybe half a dozen guns-drawn uniformed officers swarmed around the balcony. The survivalists were told to put their guns down and their hands up. Then the detective in charge came over and asked "just what the goddamn fucking hell" was the idea of scaring the shit out of half the city and endangering the lives of anybody who had the misfortune of being in or around the river.

"Couple of fags," Lynott said.

As you can imagine, the detective did not look impressed.

22

THERE WAS A DRIVE-UP PHONE TWO BLOCKS away. When I pulled in, I realized I didn't have the proper change. I had to go next door to a chain drugstore. The clerky little guy didn't look happy about breaking a five for me. I spent a college summer working retail. In that business you get to hate people, so I couldn't blame the guy.

Back in my car I called Donna.

After she said hello and before she could say anything else, I said, "There's a set of twins who just tried to get the tapes from me. They may know about you. To be safe I want you to leave there, go over to that restaurant where we've been meeting and wait for me."

A man's voice came on the other end of the phone and said, "That won't be necessary."

For an awful moment I had an image of the twins standing on either side of her. But how could they have gotten there that quickly?

Then the echoes of the voice told me who I was talking to. Chad. Her ex-husband. That emissary from *Country Gentleman* whom God had created just to make me feel inadequate.

"Hello, Chad."

"Hello, Dwyer."

Nobody would ever accuse us of sounding like long-lost buddies.

"I believe I was speaking to Donna," I said.

"I'll give you your nerve, I'll say that for you." Despite the deep rich tones of his voice, there was a prissy, judgmental quality to his voice that came naturally, I suppose, with all his money, good looks and tireless self-confidence.

"I'm not following you here, Chad."

"You've involved my wife in a murder. This is the second time. The first time her life was in danger. And now it is again."

"She's your ex-wife, Chad. Not wife."

"That's between Donna and me and is subject to change."

In the background I heard Donna say, "Oh, Chad, please let me talk to him."

"I heard that, Chad," I said.

"I'm taking my wife to our cabin for the weekend," Chad said. He used the term "wife" very freely for a man who'd dumped her for a younger woman and then reappeared only when he got bored.

"Chad, dammit, give me the phone," Donna said.

Chad covered up the receiver. Behind his hand I heard arguing. Finally the receiver sounded free, there was a pause, and Donna said, "I've listened to all the tapes now.

I'm afraid there's no really specific information. Nothing more than I told you about."

"Damn," I said.

"Just one thing. The last couple of tapes he started dating. You know, when he pressed the record button he'd say 'March nineteenth' or something. Anyway, on one of the last dates he says, 'I made the deal tonight. It will mean I get to go to California. But I'm scared that somebody will find out.' Do you know what that means?"

"No."

"I'm sorry."

There was another pause. Then, in the background, Chad said, "I really don't want to wait until these twins or whoever they are get over here, Donna."

Then Donna said to me, "I suppose we'd better be going."

"I suppose."

"You don't sound so good."

"I don't feel so good," I said.

"I'm sorry."

"I know."

"Well."

"Yeah. 'Well.'" I sounded bitter and sorry for myself. Not exactly becoming.

In the background Chad said, "Donna, for God's sake, if you can't hang up, I will."

"Good-bye, Dwyer."

"Good-bye."

Ten minutes later I stopped by Federated. Bobby Lee was typing and listening to Merle Haggard. Him I liked. When she saw me she frowned. "We said we'd call you."

"I need to get into my locker." Bobby Lee had the key that let you into the cage. With the twins after me, and God knew who else, I felt in need of the Smith & Wesson that was a holdover from my days on the force. I had stashed it there yesterday, following the murder, not thinking I'd need it.

"Why?"

"I don't need to tell you why."

"Then I don't let you in."

"We're talking about things that I happen to own."

"Tough."

"Bobby Lee. Somebody's following me."

From the doorway Becker said, "Who?" His hands glistened with glue. He was working on his model airplanes again.

"It'd take too long to explain," I said.

He shook his head. "You aren't still working on that thing that started at Channel Three, are you?"

"Afraid I am."

"Dwyer, they've got their killer. He's already in jail."

"He's not guilty."

"Then who is?"

"I'm beginning to think Fitzgerald is."

Blood flushed his face. "Are you talking about Robert Fitzgerald?" Whenever he mentioned anybody who paid him money, a kind of reverence came into his voice.

"Yes I am."

"Dwyer, do you realize he's our biggest client?"

"Yes."

"And you're still bothering him?"

"I'm trying to get to the truth."

"Doesn't that sound noble, though?" He paused and

looked at his glistening hands as if he wanted badly to wipe them on something. Then he looked back up at me. "You've forced me into a decision, Dwyer. An irrevocable one. You're fired."

"Then I can get into my locker?"

To Bobby Lee, he said, "Get Inspector Kelso on the line." Kelso was one of his buddies, a very political cop who didn't like me at all.

"I have a right to the stuff in my locker."

Bobby Lee started dialing.

"It's my locker." I sounded as if I were about five years old.

"Inspector Kelso's office, please," Bobby Lee said.

I got out of there. Fast.

He didn't come on until five o'clock, which meant that I had to hide out in the lobby until then.

When he saw me he looked afraid. He started walking away, dragging his mop and bucket as fast as he could.

I reached him and touched his elbow. "I know you're afraid. So am I. I only want to ask you a few more questions."

"They was coming in the other night. They saw me talking to you."

"They hassle you?"

"Them twins, man, they don't have to hassle you. They just give you that look." For the three dollars and change I'd given this janitor the other night, I was sure he didn't feel he owed me a beating. I didn't blame him. He put a strong hand to his face and said, "I'm scared to say anything now. They might be watching."

"Just listen to me. Please."

Condo dwellers came in and out of the lobby. It was a warm spring evening. They exuded a festiveness I wished I could share.

"You remember the kid we talked about, Stephen Chandler?"

He nodded.

"You remember the night he died?"

"I guess. But he didn't die here. He died at that half-way house."

"Falworthy, yeah. But he took the overdose here from what I can gather, and then he went back to Falworthy."

"If you say so."

"I want you to think about that night."

"All right."

"Do you remember if that aprartment had any visitors that night?"

He looked around. Fearfully. Outside the plate-glass windows that fronted the lobby an early twilight was making the world gorgeous and melancholy.

"Yeah."

I wanted to make sure he wasn't just being obliging. "Why would you have such a clear memory of that night?"

"Well, for one thing, that's the night the Chandler kid died. I saw his picture on TV. I figured the cops would ask me questions, but they didn't. 'Nother reason was the guy with the limp. I ain't likely to forget him. 'Specially the way he talked to me. Real arrogant when I asked him if I could help him."

"Tell me about him."

"I don't know. I only saw him once. Like I said, he was kinda mean, that's why I remember him and that night 'specially."

"Which means that Stephen Chandler let him in, right?"

"Yeah. He must have buzzed him up."

"Why wouldn't the twins have buzzed him up?"

He shrugged. "They was gone. Out for a good part of the night." He smiled. "They got a lot of lady friends."

"How long did he stay?"

"The guy with the limp?"

"Yeah."

He shrugged. "Half'n hour maybe."

I wanted to make sure. "Can you describe anything else about the guy?"

"Not really."

"Think about his hair."

He closed his eyes a moment. This was the worst part of police work. People just didn't notice things.

"Dark, I guess."

"Anything else?"

"About his hair you mean?"

"Yeah."

"Uh, could've been curly."

"How tall was he?"

"That's one thing I do remember."

"What's that?"

"He wasn't tall at all. He was short."

Short with dark curly hair and a limp. There couldn't be many Robert Fitzgerald look-alikes around.

He snapped his fingers. "Shit, now I remember. The kid had another visitor that night, too."

"Who?"

"This blonde."

"Before or after the guy with the limp?"

"After."

"Can you remember anything about her?"

"I couldn't see her face. I tried." He offered me a sly smile. "You know, even at my age, I like to look at the ladies."

"Short or tall?"

"Medium, I'd say."

"Younger or older?"

"Like I said, I couldn't really tell."

"But she definitely came after."

"Yeah."

"And she was blond."

"Very blond."

An image of Marcie Grant formed. I saw her walk, the way her blond hair swung with such glistening casualness.

"You 'bout done?" he said.

I nodded. "Thanks," I patted my pocket, reached down to see if I had any money.

"Forget it." He grinned. "All the money you gave me the other night, I don't have to work no more anyway." Then he nodded back to his mop and bucket. He wanted me gone.

23 TWILIGHT HAD TURNED THE CASTLE INTO something resembling its real name. Long shadows hid the plastic look of the place. When you came over the hill and looked down into the valley and saw it there, you could almost imagine what real castles must look like.

A parking attendant took my car. He was a kid, and he grinned when he saw the towel I had over the tear in my seat. It wasn't an arrogant grin. He probably had a towel over his car seat, too.

You crossed (inevitably) a moat via a drawbridge, and when you went into a gravel area where two big guys got up in armor stood on either side of a huge door, and then you entered the restaurant beneath an arch of crossed swords. This place was a kind of Disneyland for the stomach.

The drunk I saw just inside spoiled the goofy innocence of the place. He was wide and mean and he looked as if he was about to punch out the smaller man he waved a fist at.

His about-to-be victim was Hanratty, the singing weatherman.

Hanratty had apparently been coming out of the john when the guy cornered him. The guy's wife had hold of his elbow, and now the maitre d' was jumping in. Hanratty, embarrassed, kept his eyes on the floor while the man ranted.

"You think you're such fucking hot shit, don't you, pal? Well, you're nothing but a ridiculous clown." He seemed to like the taste of that phrase on his tongue. "You hear me? A ridiculous clown."

That's when another man appeared. He was big and there was a lot of efficiency in his movements. He got the drunk by the collar and the seat of the pants, and then the whole scene got funny. He wheeled the guy out while onlookers giggled and applauded.

"That's one thing the public doesn't realize," Hanratty told me ten minutes later in the dim bar. "Drunks hassle you all the time. That's why my wife will hardly go out anymore. It gets pretty miserable."

The Castle Motif was continued in here, too. The young women were dressed as skullery maids (at least that's what Yvonne DeCarlo always wore when *she* played a skullery maid), and all types of lances and shields were hung on the wall. There was a candle between us. Its wavering glow made Hanratty's Irish face look comic.

Hanratty was drinking martinis and obviously working hard at getting drunk. We were waiting for Dev Robards. By the third martini, Hanratty started to sweat. You could see it glisten there in the candlelight. "Something's wrong," he said.

"Wrong with what?"

"With Dev. He should have been here by now."

"Relax."

"He's scared. He called me several times this afternoon. Said he was afraid to be alone."

"You going to tell me?"

His fingers tightened around his drink. "Let's wait for Dev."

"We don't seem to have a lot to talk about, the two of us. No offense."

"You don't like me, do you?"

"Would you really give a shit if I said no, I don't?"

"Sure I would. I like to be liked. That's why I do all that stuff on the air. Sing those corny songs. Inside I'm still a little altar boy who likes to be told he's a wonderful kid."

Boy, was he drunk.

"So your answer's no?"

"To what?" I said.

"To liking me."

"All right, I like you."

"You're lying."

"I don't even know you. How's that?"

"You hate the songs?"

"Jesus, let's just sit here, all right?"

We tried that. It lasted about forty-five seconds. He was really freaking. He got up, catching the edge of the table against his thigh. He knocked over a couple of drinks and cursed loudly in the process.

"Sit down," I said.

"This is getting really weird."

A waitress came over. Stood and watched him. Shook her head. He'd gotten sloppy drunk very quickly. I suspected he probably drank very little, very rarely. The waitress and I got him to sit down.

He put his face in his hands. I wondered if he was crying, but there was no sound of sobbing, nor did his shoulders move even slightly. When he took his hands away, he looked stern and washed-out and almost sober. "After what we did, I'm through in this business. The kid won't be singing any more songs, let me tell you."

"You going to tell me now?"

He looked at me. I could see that not only was he drunk, he was also a little crazy. Maybe more than a little crazy. He just kept looking at me, and then he put his hands back over his face and sat there until the waitress came up with a new martini.

"I don't think he needs it," I said.

Hanratty took his hands down. He stared at the drink and smiled. "Welcome aboard," he said, and picked up the drink.

"Some admirers of yours sent it over." She nodded to the far corner of the bar, where a group of older people sat. Near them was a piano. "They've asked if you'll sing a song."

With all the bitter stuff he'd been giving me about being washed up in this business, I figured he'd say no. Instead he said, "By gum, that sounds like a darn good idea." He was the altar boy again. Praise was being promised him.

I waited in the lobby while he did it. I tried to tune in on the conversations of passersby so I wouldn't have to hear him. He did "Danny Boy" and "Red Sails in the Sunset" and "When Irish Eyes Are Smiling"; he did everything but "What a Friend We Have in Jesus." I went and emptied my bladder, stepped out into the parking lot and asked the kid if he knew who Dev Robards was (he did) and had he seen him (he hadn't) and would he run in and tell me if he did (he would).

Finally, maybe half an hour later, Hanratty came up. He was sloshing side to side, and he had lipstick all over him from where the older ladies had kissed him, and he had a grin that was obscene with self-pleasure.

"How're you?" he said.

He tried to throw his arm around me old-buddy style, but he missed and fell to the floor. Or almost fell. I got him around the stomach and pushed him through the door and told the kid to get my car, and when he came he helped me push Hanratty into it.

"Isn't that Bill Hanratty?" the kid said.

"Yeah."

"That fucker's potzed."

"Potzed," I said, roaring my engine into life. "I haven't heard that one before."

"It's a good one, don't you think?"

"It ain't bad."

I got him on the freeway and I kept the windows down and I went seventy and then eighty, and in maybe twenty miles he came around, and as soon as he did he told me to stop the car. He got out and wobbled a ways down the grassy hill. Even above the passing cars I could hear him puking.

When he came back, he looked much too old to be an altar boy.

"Where's he live?"

"Dev?" he said.

I nodded.

He told me.

"I must've really made an ass out of myself back there in the bar," he said on the way over.

"Look," I said, "everybody's under some kind of strain. You needed a release. It wasn't a big thing. You were very friendly. When I get in your mood I tend to pop people sometimes, and that's one hell of a lot worse than singing a song."

"You hit people?"

"Not exactly hit them. More like argue with them. But it has the same spiritual effect on them and me. It'd probably be better for both our sakes if I did hit them."

"Are you afraid?"

"Of what?"

"Of something having happened to him?"

"Yeah, I am."

He put his face in his hands again.

Dev Robards lived in a new townhouse. Hanratty recognized his car. "That's a bad sign, isn't it?"

"Could be," I said.

"You mind if I wait out here?"

I looked at him. I didn't understand him. I didn't care to. "Fine," I said.

The front door was locked. It took me a good ten minutes to get it open with my pick and credit card. Even then I had to punch out a small pane of glass on the side of the door to reach inside.

I didn't find him right away. I walked through a bachelor's living room that had been given over to books and some impressive lithographs, and followed a flight of stairs to a hallway at the end of which the first dark of night filled a long window.

He wasn't in the bathroom and he wasn't in the den but he was in the bedroom.

He was wearing boxer shorts and garters and he was

191

skinny and really an old bastard, and he looked funny-comic in a sad kind of way. I had no doubt that he'd been left for dead, but the way his chest rose and fell told me instantly that his would-be killer had botched the job.

I took his pulse. Faint but steady. I opened one eyelid for a look. He grunted something unconsciously. I grabbed the phone and dialed 911 and gave them the address.

Then I got down on my knees and looked over the rug. I started picking up things and looking under them and in them and around them, but I didn't find a thing. Not a thing.

He took it about the way I expected he would. At first he tried to deny it and then he got pissed off and then he got scared and then he said, "I'm probably next." He had been waiting in the car but when I'd told him about Robards he'd gotten out of the car and started pacing.

"Let's get in the car," I said.

"Did you hear me? I'm probably next."

I held the door for him. "Get in the car."

He looked behind him. Frantically. "Aren't you going to call the police or something?"

"I've already called them."

"You sure he's not dead?"

"I'm sure."

On the freeway with the windows rolled down and both of us freezing our asses off, I said, "I want you to tell me."

"Maybe you're better off not knowing."

"Don't give me that bullshit. I've been through too much to hear it. I want to know what you and Robards were up to."

He said it then and it was simple as hell. It always is when it's the truth. "We were selling secrets."

"To whom?"

"To Channel Six. Our competitor. That's who Ross, the private detective, worked for."

"What sort of secrets?"

"Oh, after we'd have a conference where we'd discuss what investigative reports we'd be doing, we'd sell what we knew to Ross and the twins, and they'd sell them to Channel Six."

I looked over at him. He was reciting all this in a flat dead voice. "Why did you do it?"

"Because we hated them, Fitzgerald and Kelly Ford and all the fucking consultants. They rule our lives, you know. They tell us how to dress, how to behave; they make fun of us to our faces. They were going to replace us—we started stealing the research reports from Kelly Ford's office over a year ago—and we could see in their private studies that we were going to be fired eventually. So we decided to make money while we could. So we sold the information."

"Did any of the information have to do with the suicide of the Chandler boy?"

"No. And that's the funny thing."

"Why is it funny?"

"That's all Ross talked about."

"Stephen Chandler?"

"Yes."

"He knew the kid, didn't he?"

Hanratty nodded. "Yes. See, Stephen was on Channel Three six months ago, after the first time he tried to commit suicide."

That I hadn't known anything about. But it made me very curious.

"So how does Ross figure in all this?"

"I'm not sure. I just know that he offered me ten

thousand dollars if I could find out what really happened to Stephen Chandler."

"What do you mean, what really happened? He committed suicide, didn't he?"

He sighed. "I'm in deep shit, Dwyer."

"Keep talking."

"Deep shit."

"Goddammit, go on."

He sighed again. "One night I went up to Ross's place."

He didn't say anything else.

I said, "Yeah. So what?"

"I started to go in, but I heard all these voices—it was the twins talking with Ross—and what I heard, well . . . The twins knew the Chandler boy pretty well. They talked about getting him laid and letting him drive their car and giving him pocket money. They had the kid do errands for them, dirty work, mostly. Nothing serious. They were trying to develop him into kind of an assistant because he had good looks and charm and a real lot of balls, I guess. A real lot."

"So?"

"So they said there was no way he committed suicide. They said somebody murdered him."

"Jesus," I said.

"What?"

"It makes sense, doesn't it?"

"What makes sense?"

"Curtis's death; somebody trying to kill Dev Robards. Because the Chandler kid wasn't a suicide at all. Somebody murdered him."

Hanratty looked out the window at the night. Trucks rolled by. Headed for the plains and then the mountains. I wanted to go with them.

"Could Ross have murdered Stephen Chandler?" I said.

"No. In his own way he was honest. He didn't know who had killed Chandler. He just knew that somebody at Channel Three had gotten the kid unconscious and purposely fed him an overdose and then dumped him back at Falworthy House." Then he said, "Shit."

"What?"

"I gotta puke again."

I wheeled over to the side of the road.

He didn't make it down the ravine this time. He stood right there off the macadam. Cars honked at him. You could hear laughter.

"You and your wife got any place you can spend the night other than home?"

"I owe her a night at a motel," he said.

"Make it tonight then."

He leaned his head in the window. He looked like an altar boy again. "He's a very nice man."

"Who?"

"Robards."

"Yeah, he is."

"You really think he's gonna be all right?"

"Yeah, but you two dipshits were way out of your league."

"You're right. You're so fucking right."

I handed him a stick of gum.

"What's this for?"

"You won't smell quite so bad when you see your wife."

"Oh. Yeah. Right. Thanks."

He was long gone. Nerves and terror had taken him away, our singing weatherman.

24

I DROVE AROUND THE PHONE BOOTH SEVERAL times before finally pulling in. Even then, still not sure, I stood in the spring night having a smoke and watching young women stroll by. For once they held no particular interest for me. Not with what was on my mind.

Finally I decided it would be best if I did what was only proper to do. As people kept reminding me, I was only a security guard. Hell, I'd been fired, so I wasn't even that.

I went into the booth and dropped in my quarter and called the precinct house number from memory. I'd dialed it a thousand times in my days as a cop. I asked for him and the man on the desk said, "Wait a minute please," and then he came back and said, "He's not in this evening. He had some time off coming."

"Thanks."

Then I tried Edelman's house. His wife, one of the truly

decent people in the universe, answered and said, "He's bowling."

"Bowling?"

She laughed. "Hard to believe, isn't it?" Then she was more serious. "Hasn't he told you about his blood pressure?"

"No."

"It's very high. The doctor's worried. They tried him on tranquilizers, but they just made him sleepy, so he's taken up bowling."

"Is the blood pressure coming down?"

"Slowly, thank God."

"Well, just mention I called if you would."

"I sure will. And it's going to be good to see you whenever that day comes around again."

I was always promising her I'd be over for dinner one day. Soon.

"Thanks," I said, and hung up.

The trailer court was dark. Just the glow of lights and TV screens in the window. When I pulled in, I saw a young couple strolling by. She had her hand stuffed deep down the back of his trousers and he had his hand stuffed deep inside her blouse. It made me smile. It would be nice to be so publicly horny again.

There were three cars parked around Marcie Grant's trailer. The last one was a new red Firebird. I took my old route, along the side of the trailer and up to the back window.

The Ayreses, identical as always in matching white shirts and black slacks, had big Mike Perry, the sportscaster, tied in a straight-back chair. Marcie Grant they had on the

197

couch. All she wore was panties. Even in the dim light you could see the odd violet glow of her eyes. What they emitted now was terror.

The place had been ransacked. It didn't take genius to know what the twins were looking for. They wanted the audiotapes that Stephen Chandler had made. Marcie was probably a long shot but these days the twins were desperate. She'd been the producer of the suicide series. She was probably worth checking out. Besides, they seemed to take genuine pleasure in their work.

I went back to my car. The other day I'd been batting flies with my son. I still had my old Louisville Slugger (Henry Aaron model) in the trunk. I went and got it, and what I did next was primitive, but it worked.

I stood behind a hedge and picked up rocks and started lobbing them at the trailer door. I had to throw several innings' worth of the damn things before I heard the conversation stop inside and one of the twins say, "Listen. What the hell's that noise.?"

There was a grave and lengthy silence, and then the other twin said, "Nothing. You're just getting spooked."

"Spooked my ass. I heard something."

"Let's just get on with it, all right? There wasn't any noise." I heard him kick over something. "Now listen, bitch, where are the tapes?"

I threw another rock. This one was a spitball. It banged off the door, and one minute later the first twin appeared. By then I was behind the door with my Henry Aaron model. It was a clean good hit and he went down first to his knees and then to his face. He crashed with the pleasing sound of something being crushed.

"Rick?" the other twin said from inside after another

minute. "Don't move, bitch." Then he too came to the door.

He surprised me. Just when I was raising Henry to do battle, he turned and saw me and leveled a .45 at my midsection.

I got him across the face. I heard things break in his nose and mouth and jaw. He looked shocked and furious, and then he collapsed next to his brother.

Inside the trailer Marcie Grant lay facedown on the couch.

Mike Perry, still tied up, watched me come into the room, his eyes widening in recognition. I went over and untied him.

"You just saved yourself some grief, pal," he said. He didn't seem unduly grateful for the fact that I might just have saved his life.

"How's that?"

"The last time you were here, you kicked me in the balls and then knocked me out."

"That's right, I did."

"So I was going to pay you back, but in light of what you did tonight, I won't."

"Gee, thanks."

Marcie got up from the couch, her wonderful breasts still naked.

"Jesus Christ," Perry said. "Haven't enough people seen your tits already?"

She ran off into the bedroom.

Two minutes later we sat around the kitchen table sharing a quart of Budweiser, and Marcie Grant told me what she knew about the Stephen Chandler case.

"All I knew was that something was wrong with the way he died. I never believed his suicide. I'd spent a lot of time with him and I knew all about his California ideas. Despite the way he talked sometimes, he was actually a reasonably happy young man. Very bright and very ambitious. But I was afraid to say anything after he died."

"Why?"

She looked at Perry and then flushed. "This is going to make me sound like a real cold-hearted bitch."

Perry said, "Tell him."

"I was afraid that if somebody had killed him, that would detract from the power of the story." She paused. "I've been nominated as producer for a major news award. It'll really help my career. Part of the power of the piece was that he actually committed suicide. But if he was murdered—"

I said, "Channel Three really profited from that story, didn't they?"

"Well, we were number two and that made us number one. That's why Channel Six got so nervous. They'd been afraid for a long time that we were going to overtake them. When we did the first piece on teenage suicide three months earlier, it helped our ratings considerably. That's why we decided to do the second part. That's when Stephen Chandler committed suidice."

"He was murdered."

They looked at each other. Then she sighed and said, "Yes. That's what I was afraid of."

"And you could have been the one who did it."

"Me? Are you crazy?" she said.

I told her about what the janitor had said. That a blond

woman had been the last person to go up and see Stephen Chandler the night he died.

"It couldn't have been me," she said.

"Why not?"

"The night the Chandler kid died, Mike and I were in Hawaii on vacation."

Perry said, "We've got lots of proof."

So that was that. My nice neat theory. I had only one other possibility. The janitor had mentioned a limping man. There didn't seem to be much doubt about who that might be. I finished my beer and stood up.

"You all right?" Marcie Grant said.

I nodded.

"He's onto something," Perry said.

"Are you really?" Marcie asked.

"I'm not sure yet," I said.

"What should we do with the twins?" she asked.

"Call the police."

"Is it all about over?" she said. She sounded weary.

"Yeah," I said. "Just about."

25 THE FIRST PLACE I LOOKED WAS KELLY Ford's. The heavy elm trees played shadows off the street again. The night smelled of apple blossoms. I walked up the wide wooden steps. I wanted to have a bouquet of yellow roses in my hand, come a-courting. It was that kind of night.

I went up the stairs to the second floor as quietly as I could. The hallway smelled of new paint. At her door I pressed my ear to the wood and listened. Nothing. Just the sounds of the apartment house. I walked down to the end of the hallway, where the window stood open. I climbed through and got on the fire-escape grating and walked over to one of her rear windows and looked inside. Darkness. Then I eased up the window and went inside.

I spent the next five minutes looking for something to make my job easier when I confronted Fitzgerald with what he'd done. I went through closets and drawers, looked under the bed, even under the sink. I had no idea what I was looking for. Under a quilt in a corner of the living room I found the hope chest, and inside the hope chest I found exactly what I hadn't been looking for. I found one thing that made me feel stupid and terrible and very, very old all at the same time.

I took it with me and left.

26

YOU COULD SEE CHANNEL 3 FROM A HALF mile away. The display lights gave it the feel of an opening-night gala year round.

I pulled into the parking lot. Right next to Fitzgerald's car. Right next to Kelly Ford's.

When the security guard saw me, he frowned. He wore a Federated uniform, and we'd been something like friends. He was maybe forty, beagle-eyed and paunchy.

"You shouldn't have come out here," he said.

"I had to."

"Why?"

"Because I figured out who poisoned that anchorman the other night."

"Jesus, Dwyer, Becker will have your nuts. When I went in there this afternoon, all he did was rant and rave about how he'd fired you."

"Fuck Becker. He's a douche bag."

"So what do you want?"

"I want in."

"No way, man. I got three kids. I got laid off the factory, my day job I mean. I just can't do it."

I sighed. Just stood there. He was right. Becker would fire him, and with so bad a rap the poor bastard wouldn't get work for years.

"Sorry," I said. "I didn't mean to put you on the spot."

"It's okay. Sorry I'm such a chickenshit."

"Hey, man, you're protecting your family. That's anything but a chickenshit."

"Yeah. I guess you're right."

I walked back to my car and got in and drove off. I parked two blocks away and came back to Channel 3 through the woods, the same path I'd taken when I was chasing Diane Beaufort the other night.

I waited in the woods until I saw somebody at the rear door. He stood there talking, saying good night to a co-worker. He stood there long enough for me to go up to him and walk past him right inside.

"Hey," he said, "you work here?"

"Yeah. In the newsroom," I said.

He and his buddy looked at me and then at each other and shrugged. I kept on walking.

I took the back stairs up to the second floor. I had a sense of ascending into deeper and deeper shadow. From below, on the first floor, I heard the buzz of the news department— people shouting, teletypes clacking, hip angry jokes evoking hip angry laughter—and then I was in the deepest shadows of all, the middle of the second floor, which had been closed down since the executives had gone home.

Exterior light fell through the tall windows as I moved

over the thick carpeting toward Fitzgerald's office. If he was watching for me, he'd have no trouble seeing me.

His office was empty.

I suspected then where I'd find him. I moved into the shadows again. The small studio was down at the west side of the building. It was a control room with banks of monitors so that Fitzgerald could see what was going on in the news studio and all four production studios.

I paused outside the door.

There was only one way to go in, the way cops go in, quickly and with surprise on their side.

I jerked open the door, and then I saw him.

He was sitting on a big futuristic swivel chair in the middle of the large oval room, which was lined on either side with banks of monitors, bright and flickering with scores of different images. His head was in his hands, and when I came in and he looked up, he didn't seem to recognize me. I used to see accident victims in this kind of shock.

Kelly Ford's greeting was far different. Before I got two steps over the threshold, she brought up a sleek new pistol and leveled it at me. "I suppose I'll have to handle him, too," she snapped at Fitzgerald.

From inside my jacket I took the blond wig I'd found in her hope chest. I threw it at Fitzgerald and then looked at her. "You killed Stephen Chandler," I said.

She came up closer. "I knew you'd figure it out." She sounded sad, very sad, and I liked her despite it all. "The other night when you were in my apartment, we were so close for a time that I got scared. I was afraid you'd be able to read my mind or something, that you'd know I'd faked the robbery at my own office to confuse the police, that I'd helped arrange Stephen's death, that it was Robert and me you were looking for." She looked down at Fitzgerald. "I wouldn't have done it if he hadn't been so weak. He was going to do it but then he backed out."

"Do what?"

"Kill Chandler. It was going to be a trick. He had gotten Stephen to agree to accept four thousand dollars and fake a suicide attempt. Take some heroin and turn himself in. Stephen went along with it. He was very intrigued by it. But Robert was going to make sure the heroin he got was so pure that he actually would die. It would make a great story. And help our ratings. Over the past year—what with his investments going bad—he's been acting pretty crazy. But I went along with him." She laughed bitterly. "Then at the last minute he didn't have the nerve to take Stephen the heroin. So I did."

I glanced down at Fitzgerald. If he was aware of what was going on, he was keeping it a secret. She followed my gaze and shot him a look that claimed whatever masculinity he had left.

"You killed David Curtis, too," I said.

"He found out. Or thought he had. Ross, the private detective, started questioning Curtis, and Curtis put things together. He threatened to expose Robert and me if we didn't make him sole anchorman. He had to be killed. Then we had to worry about his partners, the twins."

"Why did you try to kill Robards?"

She glanced up. "He's not dead?"

I shook my head.

She leaned back against a large videotape console. In the flickering light of the control room she looked her years now.

"I didn't have any choice. He saw me leave David's dressing room after I put the cyanide in the laxitive." She shook her head. "I wanted to tie up all the loose ends for Robert and me." She stared at the monitors. A terrible smile came over her face. "Just before I shot him tonight, I told him why I was doing it—and you know what he told me? That that night he'd fallen off the wagon and didn't remember me being in David's dressing room."

I tried to make sense of her words, of her, but there was no way. She had been so caught up in her need for Fitzgerald that she could have justified anything. It was a form of madness, of course, but the kind juries never buy. I looked down at Fitzgerald again. "Was he worth it all, Kelly?"

"I guess you know the answer to that," she said. She spoke in barely a whisper.

For a moment I thought she was going to break but she didn't. She kept it inside and her voice and gestures got more and more painful to watch.

"He didn't love me. He never did. Ever. But I felt so sorry for him because of his leg and because of all the pain he'd been through in his life—building his little empire here, never quite feeling as if he was the equal of any of his peers." She looked down at him again and shook her head. "I loved him so damned much."

"You could just give me the gun."

"What?" She hadn't quite heard me.

"You could just give me the gun."

"Are you afraid I'll kill you, too?"

"Yes."

"Then you don't know much about me."

"I guess I don't, after all."

"It's funny because I was about to ask you if you'd take the gun and kill me."

She was serious.

"I couldn't do that."

"Can you imagine what it's going to be like for my children and my ex-husband? All the scandal."

"They'll be all right eventually."

"In school I was always the good little girl. When they read about me in the papers, the people who grew up with me won't know what to think."

"I don't suppose they will."

"You're a very nice man. You really are."

"Thank you." And I meant it. "Don't be foolish, Kelly. You're strong. You can handle things." I was beginning to suspect what she had in mind.

"I'm not strong, that's the irony. After all this, I'm still not strong."

"Just call the goddamn police and get it over with. Give him the gun, Kelly." Fitzgerald's voice droned in the aching silence and we looked down at him as if he were Lazarus.

"Just give him the gun, Kelly," Fitzgerald said again. He didn't look natty now. Not at all.

"That's just what you'd do, isn't it, Robert? No nerve."

I could see what she was going to do and I couldn't stop her and I wasn't even sure I wanted to. She twisted the gun around to her forehead and pulled the trigger, and just like that she fell to the floor.

"My God, my God!" was all Fitzgerald could get out.

I knelt down beside her and closed my eyes so I wouldn't have to look at the mess where the top of her head had been. I took her hand and held it tightly and finally, finally I got myself to cry and goddamn but I cried, goddamn but I did.

Then I stood up and went over to where Fitzgerald sat in shock. I got him up high enough from the chair to get three good punches into his face, and then I went out to phone Edelman.

27

EDELMAN WORE HIS BIG CREPE-SOLED shoes.

Another homicide man was actually handling the case, Edelman not actually being on duty tonight, but he came in with his gloomy officiousness, and when he saw me he came over and did exactly the right thing, put his arm around me and said, "You look pretty bad, kiddo."

"I feel pretty bad." Then I said, "Your wife told me about your high blood pressure."

"I'll be all right."

"I worry about you, Edelman, you crazy bastard. I really worry about you."

"Yeah, well," he said, "I worry about you, too." Then he grinned. "Was it you who worked over Fitzgerald?"

"Yeah."

"You did nice work." Then he smiled and went away again.

28 THREE DAYS LATER MY AGENT CALLED AND said I got the dinner-theater part, and then another security company called and asked if I'd like to come to work for them, and then my kid called and said he'd gotten a B-minus average, which, given the way both of us hated school of any kind, was a damn good report card.

I played some basketball, and finally got Becker to give me my locker stuff back, and stared at the phone a lot.

Friday it rained, and Friday she called.

"How're you doing?"

"I'm doing okay. How're you doing?"

"Oh," she said, "I guess you could say I'm doing okay, too." Then she asked about the case, and I told her.

"How's Rex?"

"I slapped him last night."

"Are you serious?"

"Yes."

"How did he take it?"

"He got hysterical, actually. He said I was a, quote, 'stupid neurotic bitch and that I should get out of his fucking office.' Unquote."

"Good old Rex."

"God, I miss you, Dwyer."

"Yeah, but do you miss me more than you miss Chad?"

"I don't have to miss Chad. He's always either cruising around my apartment or having flowers sent over. My place looks like a mortuary."

"So what're you going to do?"

"Take a little vacation?"

"Where?"

"Mexico."

"For what?"

"To think things through. I've got to get rid of him, Dwyer. I really do."

I'd gone through a similar love affair once. I know how difficult it can be.

"You don't have to be faithful or anything," she said.

"You'd like me to be faithful, huh?"

"Well . . ."

"How long do I have to be faithful?"

"Well, Jesus, Dwyer, if we got married you'd have to be faithful forever."

"Well, how long do I have to be faithful this time?"

"What an asshole."

"How long?"

"Six days. Max. I'll probably get dysentery and have to come back after three. But six days max."

"Six days max I can be faithful."

She laughed. "God, I love you, Dwyer, I really do."

"You make me crazy."

"I know that. I make me crazy, too."

"Take care of yourself, kiddo."

"Yeah," she said, "you too."

The next call I got was a real surprise. It was a moving company, the front office, saying I'd been listed as a job reference for a Miss Bobby Lee Davies.

"You're shitting me," I said.

"I beg your pardon?" asked the rather prim woman. "I must have the wrong number." And with that she hung up.

Two minutes after that another call came through. The country music in the background was a good indication of whom I was about to talk to.

"Hi, Jack."

She'd never called me Jack before. Ever. And I didn't want her to do it again, either.

"You're going to get a call this afternoon. I just need a teensy favor."

"I got the call. And no favors, Bobby Lee. Have your sugar daddy Becker do you some favors."

"He fired me."

"What?"

"True-blue, Dwyer. He fired me. Said I was getting too pushy. Can you imagine?"

"Oh, no, Bobby Lee, I could never imagine you being too pushy."

But my sarcasm was lost on her.

"Do you know how many monthly payments I've got, Dwyer? I've got payments on my GTO, on my VCR, on my stereo, at the kennel for my German shepherd, for the Merle Haggard Golden Collection I'm buying. . . ." She sounded as if she might cry. "I can't ask my daddy to help me anymore because he'll just say it serves me right for giving myself to a married man. He'll just say I should have learned my lesson before."

"Before?"

"I can't help it, Dwyer. I just can't seem to fall in love with anybody who isn't wearing a ring." Then she paused. "Jack, I heard tell that you've gone and got yourself a job at a new security company."

"Bobby Lee, Jesus Christ."

"I'll thank you, Jack, as much as I respect you, to refrain from taking the Lord's name in my presence. As soon as Earl kicked me out, the first place I headed was back to the Baptist church. There'll be no more sin for this young lady."

A week and a half later, Bobby Lee, repentant as shit, started work as the receptionist at my new place of employment, the American Security Agency.

About the Author

Edward Gorman has been in the advertising business for twenty years. He has published short fiction and criticism in magazines from coast to coast. He lives and works in Cedar Rapids, Iowa, where he now runs his own advertising agency. He is the author of ROUGH CUT and NEW, IMPROVED MURDER.

Case after case of
Mystery, Suspense and Intrigue...
ERLE STANLEY GARDNER'S
PERRY MASON MYSTERIES